I0654290

Haunted West Virginia

More Scary Ghost Stories and Creepy Folk Tales to Keep you Up at Night

Written and illustrated by Jannette Quackenbush

Copyright © 2025 by Jannette Quackenbush

ISBN-13: 978-1-940087-73-3

Jannette Quackenbush is an author of over 50 books, folklorist, naturalist, and paranormal researcher. She focuses on ghost stories, folklore, and hiking trails in the Appalachian and southern U.S. Known for her engaging storytelling, she has published many works on local legends and haunted places. Her project, "Dark Journeys with Jannette," features guided hikes where participants explore haunted sites and learn about the region's folklore, connecting them to the rich cultural history and stories of the area. People always ask me, "Do you believe?" And here is how I feel, "Everybody is a skeptic until they experience something out of the norm. Then, all of a sudden, they realize there is more out there to discover, and they become part of this big community of others whose eyes are open to the unknown. And they want to know more, see more, adventure more. Do I believe? Well, I'd certainly rather be racing out to be with the believers, the adventurous ones who get out and explore. You can be among this community too—just get out there!"

Rawhead and Bloody Bones
(Logan and Boone County)

"Say your prayers, cross your chest, and tuck your toes in tight —or Rawhead'll find you before the morning light."

Something Best Left Unspoken

He was a lumpish, headless thing, all rotten sinew, and yellow bone, dragging his own gnawed-off skull by the stringy, blood-clotted hair. His joints cracked when he moved, wet with the slop of things better left unspoken. His name was only whispered—and only in the safe hours of daylight —Rawhead and Bloody Bones.

Oh, he was horrid!

Where the Dark Lives Thickest

He made his home where the dark lived thickest—down in the sour, dripping throats of abandoned mine shafts and the muggy-scented root cellars that families built and forgot. In the breathing dirt, beneath sagging floors and loose stones, Raw Head crouched in the gloom, biding his time.

Waiting for Mama to send you down the cellar steps for a couple of Ball Mason jars of pickled eggs or cabbage for supper.

As little feet tip-toe-tip-toed down each stair step—quiet, careful, praying not to wake what slept beneath—Raw Head thrust out his bloodied, detached head from the murk. Holding open the lazy lids with finger and thumb, he peered out, a dribble of thick spit sliding down its chin.

If the child had done some bad deed that day—a lie, a stolen sweet, a prayer left unsaid—Raw Head would make a soft, mewling sound, almost pleased.

Through the Cracks and Grates

He could slip into homes through the tiniest crack — a warped board, a broken seal, a window foolishly left ajar for a breath of night air.

A single creak would betray him—just one. Then a wet whisper slithering out from under the bed.

"What have you got those big eyes for?" he'd croon, voice like damp bark peeling off a dead tree. "To see your grave," he'd answer himself in a voice that sounded like dirt pouring slowly into a coffin.

Sometimes, he peeked through the cellar grates, his rotted skull swinging gently from his hand, one empty socket squinting, the other leaking something black and syrupy. Waiting. Watching. Smiling without a mouth.

The Scent of a Prayerless Child

He sniffed the air, dragging the reek of mildew, earth, and blood deep into whatever rotten thing pulsed inside his ribcage.

He searched for the smell of naughty children—the ones who hadn't knelt to pray, who hadn't crossed themselves before the dark swallowed the world outside their windows.

And if he found them...

Oh, if he found them...

He'd reach up with a damp, skeletal hand, just a whisper of bone against the night, and tug at the sheet until a pink toe poked free into the cool night air.

First, a nibble.

A tickle.

Then a chew. A wet, crunching gnaw.

Too Late to Scream

And if a child woke to see that hulking shadow crouched by the bedside — all slime, slop, and tattered grave cloth — it was already too late.

Because Raw Head didn't just nibble toes.

No, some nights, when the hunger gnawed deeper than usual, he'd open that ruined gash across the base of his neck—that maw ringed with broken teeth—and swallow them whole, blanket and all.

Their tiny, muffled screams stuffed down into his hollow belly, where they would echo forever.

Where no prayer could reach.

What Morning Brings

Come morning, there'd be nothing left but a drag mark across the dusty floorboards.

Maybe — if you looked hard enough—a single, wet, gnawed footprint stamped on the cellar door.

And a house that would never again smell clean, no matter how hard you scrubbed.

Because once Raw Head and Bloody Bones came inside, he never truly left.

The Hag of Hawk's Nest
(Fayette County)

"If you see the old Hag on the rise,
Today is the day you are going to die."

A Precipice for the Damned

There are steep, ragged cliffs brooding over Hawk's Nest in the New River Gorge, where the old trees knot their roots into the bones of the earth and the winds howl like things half-mad. Ancient paths snake through the woods there — beaten thin by the feet of the doomed and those foolish enough to follow.

She Who Walks the Edge

For hundreds of years, the locals spoke in low tones of a figure seen pacing the high cliff's teeth-thin edges.

It was a woman draped in black homespun, her skirts tattered and moving as if caught underwater.

Her face was never clear.

Only her eyes—blacker than burned coal—smoldered through the mist.

Old-timers said she carried a curse.

Those who dared look too long into her staring eyes would feel "the vertigo" seize them—sudden, gut-wrenching dizziness so fierce it pitched men screaming off the cliffs like stones.

They whispered she could find you even if you stayed on the trail.

A slip. A stumble.

Then, nothing but the crack of your skull against the rocks below.

The Red Thread Against the Dead

The only protection lay in a thin red bracelet made of thread tied tight around the wrist.

A warning tether.

A desperate prayer.

But even then, the lucky ones only caught a glimpse of her—hovering like a shadow stitched into the rocks, waiting.

Nachtalp: The Nightmare Spirit

When the German settlers came into the gorge, they knew her for what she was.

Not a ghost.

Not a woman.

But a Nachtalp.

A creature born of nightmares—its name twisted from the old words: "Nacht," for night, and "Alp," for goblin.

At night, it did not walk the cliffs.

It came into the cabins.

It slid its skeletal weight onto the chests of sleepers, stealing their breath and stuffing terror into their lungs.

Those who lived through it spoke of waking paralyzed, their mouths open in silent screams, a shadow sitting astride them, grinning with a mouth full of broken nails.

And those who didn't wake—they were found cold and stiff in their beds by morning, their faces twisted into rigid grimaces of pure horror, as if they had fallen a thousand feet in their dreams.

Beware the Hawk's Nest at night, for in those woods, the ground remembers blood.

The cliffs remember screams.

And the Hag of Hawk's Nest is still waiting, black-eyed and smiling, to finish what the fall could not.

The Changeling Bogs of Cranberry Glades
(Pocahontas County)

"The good folk came in the night, and they Have stolen my bonny wean away; Have put in his place a changeling, A weashy, weakly, wizen thing!" Dora Sigerson

Where the Soil Breathes Wrong

The settlers came to Cranberry Glades in the 1700s, drawn by the thick forests, the heavy air, and the glitter of deer trails winding through the mist.

By the 1800s, logging camps gnawed at the old-growth red spruce and hemlock forests— but the bogs at the heart of the Glades stayed untouched.

They were too wet. Too soft. And too feared.

The men who dared stray too deep into the mist spoke of whispers that followed them, feet that sank too easily into the earth—and hands, pale as mushrooms, tugging from below.

Snatched by the Good Folk

Early on, the old-timers warned: Linger too long among the cranberry thickets and black pools, and the Good Folk would find you.

But these weren't the pretty fairies of painted books.

No, the ones that lived here were wild and cruel, their mouths wide and wet with hunger.

They snatched children with soft, blameless souls—pulling them down into the roots and muck—and left something else in their place.

A changeling.

A sickly, wide-eyed thing with fingernails sharp as thorns and a breath that stank of swamp rot.

Its skin stayed damp and cold no matter how many fires you built.

Its teeth grew long and pointed.

And its appetite...its appetite was monstrous.

Some said you could hear them gnashing their teeth in the cradle at night, dreaming of marrow and blood.

Testing the Child

Mothers had their ways of testing, whispered down from the old country.

Take a cracked eggshell. Boil it in plain water.

And watch. If the baby so much as laughed—or worse, if it spoke—it was no child of yours.

It was something old and starved wearing the skin of your baby.

What the Bogs Still Hide

The Glades are quieter now.

The logging camps are long gone; the stumps rotted into mounds.

But when the mist rises heavy off the bogs in the fall, old folks still nail iron horseshoes to their doors, still whisper charms into the cradle.

Because the Good Folk haven't left.

They're still watching the paths through the cranberry thickets, still sniffing the air for warm, easy hearts.

Still waiting for someone foolish enough to stay too long.

Gray Wailer of Booger Hole
(Clay County)

"Wailing low and dragging red,
She'll leave you cold and full of dread."

Blood in the Hollow

Tucked deep in the hills of Clay County lies a hollow known as Booger Hole. What happened there in the late 1910s still chills the bone. Between 1917 and 1918, the hollow grew rotten with fear. A string of brutal, unsolved murders and vanishings crossed the land like a sickness.

Neighbors found bodies rotting in wells.

Cabins torched black with no living soul inside.

Paths where the earth drank up men whole—and no answers ever came.

She Walks Before Death

The locals began to murmur of her.

The Gray Woman.

Barefoot.

Silent.

Dragging a blood-soaked rag across porch floors slick with dew.

She never knocked.

She never spoke.

She just stood there, dripping and watching.

And by morning, someone in that house would be dead.

Some said she was the ghost of a murdered widow, done in by a jealous husband or a squatter itching for land.

Others swore she was a banshee, a death-spirit carried to these hills from the old country, come wailing for fresh souls.

Whatever she was, her meaning was clear: If you saw her, death was already coming.

A Town on the Edge

The killings weren't whispered campfire tales — they were grim, documented fact. Contemporary newspapers like the Charleston Daily Mail and Clay County Free Press wrote it plainly: Bodies found in dry wells.

Cabins gutted by fire. Travelers vanishing mid-step.

No suspects.

No trials.

No peace.

The terror grew so thick that the men of Clay County formed a vigilante band and posted their own warning in 1917: "We have pledged our lives to drive these murderers from our county or kill them... If they don't leave, we will get them."

This was no ghost story.

This was blood justice.

The Curse of Booger Hole

"Booger" was an old Appalachian word for ghost, monster, nightmare—and Booger Hole had long been feared, long before the killings painted its soil red.

The name stuck. The fear stayed. And even after the murders faded into time, old folks kept their doors barred tight come dusk.

To this day, Clay County families will still tell you: If you see the Gray Woman—don't answer. Don't speak. Don't even breathe.

Wilson Douglas and the Wailing Woman

The famous fiddler and storyteller Wilson Douglas knew Booger Hole's ghost wasn't just a story. He lived it.

In 1932, as a boy of eleven, Wilson moved to the hollow. One day, while squirrel hunting a narrow animal trail, he saw her. He told it like this: It rained that morning, but now the sun glistened on the dripping leaves. Wilson stopped to bask in the warmth, standing along a faint trail worn by moonshiners and deer.

Then—the snap of a twig.

He looked up and saw a woman coming toward him.

Not hurrying.

Not stumbling.

Just floating forward, her coal black hair dragging the ground behind her, her face buried in her hands.

"She was a-dyin'," Wilson said later. "I never heard nothin' so pitiful in my life."

At first, he thought she was one of the women from the valley's moonshine still camps who was weeping over some terrible fight. He waited.

He thought when she drew even with him, he'd cough, shuffle, make some noise to show he was there.

But as she neared—he saw her feet had never touched the earth.

And when she was nearly upon him, she rose into the air and vanished, mid-wail.

Wilson never went hunting alone in Booger Hole again.

If You See Her...

If you hear wailing in the woods near Booger Hole — don't follow it.

Don't look for it.

Because what walks those paths still weeps for blood.

And she's always looking for another door to darken.

Corpse Candles in Coal Hollow
(Logan and Mingo County)

"If the flame turns blue and walks your way,
Get gone by dark — or there you'll stay."

The Day the Mountain Screamed

On December 6, 1907, the Monongah mines — No. 6 and No. 8—tore open with a sound like the earth screaming. Methane gas swelled in the blackness. Coal dust danced in the air like dry snow. Then flame. Then collapse. The ground heaved. Men screamed. And then the mountain swallowed 362 souls in one breath.

The ones who didn't die outright burned in the shafts.

Those deeper down suffocated slowly, clawing at the walls with blackened fingers.

Some were found days later — their hands chewed down to bone.

What the Fire Left Behind

The shafts of Coal Hollow never healed.

They stayed dark, wet, and gas-choked, yawning open like the mouths of the dead.

The miners who returned—the ones who dared—said the tunnels were never quiet again.

It wasn't just the creaking beams or the groaning rock.

It was the feeling of being watched.

Then came the lights.

Corpse Candles in the Smoke

Tiny blue flames began to appear at the mouths of the sealed tunnels.

Flickering low. Creeping slow. Not lanterns.

Not tricks. Watchers.

The Welsh miners had a name for them—*Canwyll Corff*: corpse candles. Old country omens.

Spirits that float just ahead of the dying. To see one flicker near a shaft meant death would come before the next shift's end.

The Flickering Omen

The lights didn't dance like will-o'-the-wisps.

They drifted. Patient. Deliberate. As if they were searching.

One miner said he watched a blue flame snake along the rails and disappear into a sealed shaft—and within hours, the roof gave out and took three more men.

They say sometimes, when the wind is still, you can hear the quiet hiss of those lights moving through the coal dust, and feel the heat on your face...like breath from something long dead.

Don't Look at the Light

Some men refused to work if the lights were seen the night before.

Others carried charms or muttered prayers in Welsh, though few would say what they meant.

The last watcher ever seen, they say, appeared in the middle of the track at twilight—a blue flame hovering inches from the ground.

The foreman spat at it. Laughed.

He never made it to morning.

The Hollow Never Lets Go

Today, the shafts are sealed.

The stone paths overgrown.

But the hollow remains cold and too quiet.

And if you ever wander near Coal Hollow, and the dusk grows strange—don't follow the light.

Don't chase it. Don't look it in the eye.

Because the watchers are still there, drifting slow like breath from a buried throat.

And if you see one...

It's not to warn you. It's to claim you.

The dead don't burn alone.

Curse of Black Lucy
(Greenbrier County)

"If the frogs go still and your lantern dies,
best ride fast 'fore the shadow flies."

The Witch in the Hollow

After the war, she came walking. "Black Lucy," they called her—a freedwoman who kept to herself along the twisting banks of Sinking Creek, where the trees pressed in tight and the holler never quite dried out. She was a healer to some. A hag to others. But all agreed: she had knowledge that didn't come from scripture.

Locals whispered that Lucy had been wronged by a powerful white family—cheated, humiliated, and left with nothing but her land and her secrets.

She lived alone. And she died alone.

But not quietly.

The Cattle Rot and the Night She Died

The night she passed was unnatural.

No moon.

No wind.

The woods stood too still.

And by morning, a prominent man's cattle — fat and strong the day before — were found bloated and rotted in the field, their eyes gone, their mouths twisted open like they'd choked on the air.

People talked.

Some said the beasts had caught a sickness.

Others said they'd been hexed.

But all remembered that Lucy had cursed that man's name in public two winters earlier—and swore he would "bleed through his herd."

She was buried without ceremony.

The ground wouldn't settle right.

The Shadow on the Road

It began soon after.

Just before dusk, drivers saw a long black shadow crossing the road—not walking, not gliding, but stretching, dragging, like something pulled across the sky.

Horses that saw her bolted in blind terror.

Wagons crashed.

Men fell sick that night and never healed right.

Some said they saw a woman with twisted hands and burning eyes in the woods, muttering to herself, dragging a bundle of rags behind her.

Children grew pale.

Crops soured.

Dogs refused to pass her stretch of the road.

The Curse That Stuck

The elders say Black Lucy's wrath didn't fade with time—it deepened.

That she walks Sinking Creek still, angry and unburied in her heart.

She doesn't speak.

She doesn't scream.

But her eyes will find you if you ride too late, and her shadow will reach you before you even know to pray.

Stillness Means She's Near

If you ever pass that way, listen close.

If the frogs go quiet and the leaves stop rustling, if the wind holds its breath and your skin goes cold— don't stop.

Don't look.

Because Black Lucy walks at dusk.

And what she didn't get in life, she'll take in death.

Doppelgänger of Sugar Grove
(Pendleton County)

"If you see your shadow walk ahead,

turn and run or soon be dead."

Shadows That Walk Before You

Near Sugar Grove, there's a stretch of road that the locals won't walk at dusk.

Not for money. Not for blood.

Because sometimes, out there in the trees—you see yourself.

Not just a shadow. Not a trick of light.

But *you*, striding just ahead in the failing light—your same coat, your same limp, your same ragged breath in the cold.

And if *that* double turns and looks at you—you won't live to see the next full moon.

A Sign That Death Has Claimed You

Old people said the doppelgänger wasn't a ghost—it was a warning.

A soul echo. A borrowed face. It only came when your death had already been written down.

Not to kill you, but to mark you.

You could scream. You could pray.

But if you saw yourself walking where you had not walked yet—your days were numbered.

Breaking the Curse

But there was a way—a terrible old custom whispered from grandmother to grandson in the dark.

If you saw your double: Immediately turn your clothes inside out.

Walk backward for nine full steps.

And do not speak. Not a word. Not even a whisper.

If you did all that, just maybe the road would forget your name. Just maybe, the death would pass you by.

Two Graves for One Soul

They say a man named Avery Dunn was the last to see it.

Came home pale as birch bark, mumbling and shaking, his boots soaked with something that wasn't rain.

Tried the old trick, turned his coat, and stumbled back nine steps into a ditch.

Didn't speak for two days.

But he lived.

Two weeks later, a man identical to Avery was found dead in the same spot—face down in the brush, bones snapped like twigs.

No one could tell if it was Avery... or the other one.

Don't Follow Yourself

So, if you ever walk the Sugar Grove road and see a shape ahead— same clothes. Same gait. Same twitch in your right shoulder...

Don't follow.

Don't call out.

And don't let it turn.

Because if it does —

your soul's already been claimed.

Old Man Fire Eyes
(Nicholas County)

"If Fire-Eyes comes and you say no—
He'll light your bones before he goes."

The One Who Comes With the Storm

In Nicholas County, he comes when the thunder shakes the roots. When the lightning ruptures the sky. And rain is pouring from black clouds.

When the night air smells like sulfur, and the frogs' trills are deafening, you might find him waiting at a crossroads—thin as a broom handle, pale as cold fire ash.

He has two burning coals where his eyes should be.

They call him Old Man Fire-Eyes.

He never speaks aloud.

He just stands there, rain pouring down his shoulders like blood from a fresh deep wound, holding out a hand and asking one thing: "Got fire?"

Matches. A hot coal. A lantern flame. A lighter.

Even a struck spark from flint will do.

But if you tell him no...your house will burn before the week has passed. And most likely, you'll go with it.

Flames for Flesh

No one knows where he came from.

Some say he was once a miner who burned to death deep in the seams of a gas-choked shaft.

Others say he was never human at all—just a fire spirit born from the breath of coal and lightning, a soul-less entity looking to harm.

Those who looked into his ember eyes say they saw scorched timber, charred corpses, and homeplaces nothing more than a blackened pile of burnt lumber.

He smiles occasionally, they say—but his teeth are too numerous, too dark, too sharp. He exhales dark smoke, which also curls from his nostrils.

Once, a man in Richwood turned him away, claiming he didn't believe in superstitions.

Three days later, his cabin caught fire in the dead of night.

His screams could be heard all the way down Cranberry Ridge. He burned to ashes.

Gone. Not a trace remained.

The Loup-Garou Connection

Some of the old families — especially those who traced their roots to French fur traders or Acadian stock—had a different name for him: Loup-Garou.

Not a wolf exactly, but a curse with a body. A shape that walks in a man's skin when wrath or sin have boiled too long. A creature that would transform into an animal, especially during the full moon.

In old French lore, the loup-garou asked for help—fire, food, or prayers.

And if you refused?

He'd bring ruin to your home and soul.

In Nicholas County, the tale stuck—twisted into coal and storm and flame.

Old Man Fire-Eyes didn't shift shape... but he sure wasn't human either.

How to Break the Curse

If you give him fire, you're safe. For now.

If you've nothing to offer, turn your pockets inside out. Step backward three times. Don't speak. Not even a whisper. And pray the flame doesn't follow you home.

His Light Still Burns

People still claim to see him—standing at three-way forks where dirt meets gravel and trees lean too close.

They say you'll feel him first—a sudden heat at your back. A matchbook going damp in your coat.

Then, the soft hiss of breath.

Then, the question: "Got fire?"

And If You Don't...

If your hearth goes cold that night, watch the floorboards — they may breathe.

If your lantern flickers and the wind doesn't stir, get out fast.

Don't gather.

Don't look back.

Because Old Man Fire-Eyes never leaves empty-handed.

He always takes something with him.

What's left behind clings to the ashes—something hollow, something screaming. A splinter of your soul scorched into the charred remains, trapped there, whispering to be put back together so it can crawl free.

Leech-eyed Boy of Mudlick Hollow

(Lincoln County)

"Red-eyed boy with a leech's stare,
Don't speak his name or breathe his air.
Cross three times if his scream you hear—
Or dig a grave for someone dear."

A Face Like Glass, Eyes Like Leeches

They called him Joszef, born red-eyed and slick as a peeled peach in the back room of a coal camp shack.

He lived just outside Mudlick Hollow along the waters of Back Fork. His folks were quiet people—Hungarian immigrants, old-country Catholic and full of strange mutterings, who kept black crucifixes over every door and ashes in every jar.

No one saw the mother again after the birth. They say she went mad from what came out of her.

Or died.

Or something worse.

The Death Talker

Joszef didn't cry like other babies.

He just stared.

His face was smooth—too smooth.

No eyebrows. No crease.

His skin caught the firelight like mirror glass, and his eyes... his eyes were dark red, like leeches emerging from the warm, swampy ponds created by creek overflow after rain.

By age four, he was speaking to no one. Then he began to see angels in the trees.

By age six, he was whispering in a raspy, deep voice about things no one had told him:

who would die,

when the barn would burn, where the buried bones were under the black walnut tree.

He'd sit beneath the apple trees and talk to people who weren't there—said he saw "angels with tree limbs for arms" and "white wolves with baby hands in their mouths."

Storm Day Curse

The townsfolk started to fear him.

Some blamed him for the stillbirths.

Some blamed him for the cattle dying.

One woman swore she heard him laughing during her husband's funeral, even though nobody saw him there.

Then came the storm.

A freak lightning strike split the old cornfield wide.

Joszef had been out in it—watching the sky with his arms raised, giggling, dancing macabre with knee-jerking steps.

When they found him, he was blackened, curled like burnt paper, but his eyes were still open. Struck by lightning, he was.

Eyes leech red.

Still watching.

The Hollow That Doesn't Heal

They buried him near the mouth of the hollow, but the preacher refused to perform the full rites.

Some claimed he started the ritual, but suddenly, terror appeared in his eyes. He stopped, closed his Bible, and walked away, mumbling something raspy and deep under his breath.

Since then, people swear the rain hits different there—comes sideways and rancid, smelling like a dead animal along the roadway.

A fog curls up suddenly and seeming from nowhere.

Livestock and pets avoid the mouth of the hollow, acting jittery before bolting in panic.

And during thunder, folks hear a child's scream, high and rising like water boiling in a kettle.

They say if you hear it, you must cross yourself three times— once for the body, once for the blood, and once for whatever soul he might've had. If you don't, someone you love will die before the ground dries. Or someone in your family will bear a child with leech-red eyes.

Eyes in the Laurel
(Greenbrier County)

"The eyes that shine but never blink,

Will drag you down before you think."

Where the Trees Watch You Back

The mountain laurel grows thick in Greenbrier County—hardy, twisting trees with pink bell-shaped flowers and roots that grip the hillsides like claws.

Their branches knot together in dense, choking walls. Rabbits, foxes, and opossums hide in them.

So do worse things.

In the thickets near Big Draft, there's a stretch of brush that no hunter walks after dark.

They say something waits there — not an animal, not a ghost—but something crouched and watching.

You'll know it by the eyes. Two glowing eyes — low to the ground, like a child crouching, unblinking and wrong.

They don't flicker. They don't twitch.

They just stare.

Locals call them Death Lights. Or Laurel Watchers.

Don't Stare Back

If you see them, turn away. Fast. Even though you don't want to. Don't let your curiosity get the best of you. Don't creep forward, awestricken. Don't stare.

Because if you look too long, the woods will change.

You'll feel it—the air go thick, the brush pull tighter, the sound of leaves breathing.

Some say the trees bend in behind you.

Others say the path you came in on just vanishes.

And if you keep looking, you go mad.

Not all at once. Not loud. Just slow.

Like sap filling your head and pressing you silent.

The Witch's Bait

Old-timers claimed the eyes belonged to a witch's changeling—a child stolen long ago, hollowed out, and planted in the brush like a trap.

It crouches there, silent, waiting for you to come close enough.

They say it grins when you step toward it—but its mouth isn't where it should be.

And if you touch it?

You'll never leave those woods in one piece.

Twistabout Ridge

(Clay County)

"Twistabout road, twistabout track,
What goes missing don't come back."

Where the Road Ends

There's a place in Clay County where the road gives up.

It's called Twistabout Ridge, and it earns its name.

It starts paved, winding, and narrow through the hills above Procious. But the further you go, the more it crumbles—first to busted asphalt, then gravel, then a rough dirt scar.

Eventually, it disappears altogether into woods too thick and too quiet, leaving only trail, bramble, and breath.

People always lived along that ridge.

But something has always lived in the mud.

The Haunted Hole

A mud hole sits at a low gap where two creeks meet—near a place the sun forgets.

It never dries.

It never drains.

Some say it was once a watering path for livestock. Others say it was once a tree-hung graveyard, fed by rope and rot. But what's true is this: People see things there. Hear things. Lose things.

The Dog That Floated

Addie Dawson grew up along Twistabout.

One afternoon, she was walking with her two boys and their dog, Cub, when the animal darted off after a rabbit.

A moment later, she passed the mud hole—and there Cub was, floating in midair above it, paws outstretched, legs stiff like death had frozen him.

She blinked. So did the boys.

Cub hovered weightlessly above the muck, like a ghost caught in a trap. Then he vanished, only to reappear from the woods on all fours, as if nothing had happened. He bounded up to the boys, looking spooked.

When the boys asked Addie if she had seen what they saw, she fibbed and spoke, "No, I didn't see anything at all." But she did.

The Rider Who Wasn't Alone

Walter White—an old horseman—not the kind to spook—was riding past the hole late one night.

Moonless. Pitch-black.

His horse jolted, and something cold and wet settled onto the back of the saddle behind him.

He didn't turn.

He couldn't.

The hair on his neck rose, and he felt breath on his shoulder, thick and mold-wet.

He rode harder, blind in the dark, until he saw the lights of his home.

That's when it slid off—a shape like a slug of skin and rope—and crawled back into the brush.

The Dare

A group of young churchgoers once dared each other to speak to the thing in the hole.

"Come and get me, ghost!" one girl called.

A second joined in, laughing.

But then a white, wet thing like a sheet soaked in meat slithered out of the hole, wrapping around their ankles with cold fingers.

They screamed and kicked.

But it tangled them so tight they could barely move.

They got away.

But they never laughed at Twistabout again.

The Hanging Mud

Some say the mud hole was born of a hanging.

During the war, a troop of Confederate soldiers found a Union spy in their ranks.

They strung him up from an oak near the road—left him to rot. No burial. No prayer.

When the rope finally gave way, the body dropped—plop—face-first into the wet black earth.

When the wind is high, folks swear they hear a body fall. Even when there's no tree. Even when there's no wind.

The Pregnant Curse

Years later, a man settled on Twistabout with his wife and her housemaid.

Both women were pregnant.

And both women, folks whispered, were carrying his children. A young midwife came to tend them.

Then, the wife died.

Then the maid died.

Then the midwife began to swell with child herself—and she married the man not long after.

But the ghost of the dead wife wasn't done.

They say her spirit walks the ridge road on full-moon nights, a white shape with a swollen belly and a purple tongue hanging from strangled lips.

The midwife never carried a child to term.

She buried her stillborns in a cemetery atop the ridge.

And now—when the moon is high—you can hear them crying. Not in cribs. In the dirt.

Widow Ratliff's Thorn Fence
(Raleigh County)

"Thorn to thorn and gate to gate,
The widow waits to twist your fate."

There's a patch of land in Raleigh County that still won't grow straight.

They say it belonged to a woman named Cordelia Ratliff, a widow who lived there near the end of the 1800s.

People called her peculiar. She kept thick curtains over her windows—never opened them.

When she did appear outside, she wore her black mourning clothes like a second skin, even years after her husband's death.

But it was her fence that people feared.

Cordelia built it herself—from twisted black hawthorn, the kind with thorns as long as your finger and hard as bone. She wove it tight around her home like a cage and locked the gate every night at sundown, claiming it kept witches out.

She said they came crawling through the brush after dark, whispering in strange tongues, sniffing for warmth. Sometimes, she said they didn't come alone.

The Thing Behind the Gate

Cordelia never let anyone in.

Neighbors whispered that if you passed too close after sunset, you'd hear her talking — but not to herself.

To something else.

Something on the other side of the fence.

One boy dared to peek through the hawthorn. He said he saw a shape behind her, crouched in the corner of her porch. Its mouth hung open. Its limbs were wrong.

He never spoke again after that night.

The Ghost in Black

When Cordelia died — and she did die alone — nobody claimed the house.

No one even buried her proper. They say her body lay in the parlor for two days before someone brave enough stepped through the thorn gate.

Then, the sightings began.

A black figure, draped in mourning cloth and soaked with rot, seen pacing the old fence line, whispering curses in a tongue no one could place.

They said the smell of wet rags followed her, and where she passed, the wind died.

Sometimes, if you stood too close, you'd feel your vision pull sideways as if the very air warped around her.

Clawed From the Inside

The children — they didn't listen.

One by one, they crept to the fence to dare each other to touch it.

The next morning, they woke screaming, their arms welted and ripped from within, like something had clawed them from under the skin.

No one heard birdsong in that yard again.

No squirrels. No dogs. Even the trees looked sick — their limbs twisted and twitching, as if they ached to move but couldn't.

As WPA folklorist R.S. Carpenter wrote in his 1938 field notes: "Ratliff's land is shunned as if salt were scattered there. Even the dogs won't walk it."

They Still See Her

The house fell into ruin, but the thorn fence still stands. Rotten, yes — but not gone.

And some nights, when the moon is low, and the fog sits heavy, you can still hear her pacing there.

Mourning clothes dragging in the leaves.

Whispering things that burrow into your dreams.

Tommyknockers
(Putnam County)

"He taps to warn, or taps to curse—
And only the dead can tell which is worse."

Tommyknockers

In the deepest cuts of Buffalo Ridge, where the rock breathes and the lanterns sweat, miners speak of things older than the coal.

They call them Tommyknockers.

Deep Folk.

Or just the Knockers.

They Knock Before the Earth Takes You

Miners say the Knockers live inside the walls — not behind them, but inside — curled in the stone like beetles in marrow.

You'll know they're near when the air thickens.

When your ears ring, and your pick hits stone but makes no sound. Then comes the knocking.

Seven sharp raps echoing down the shaft like a warning... or a countdown.

No one swings.

No one breathes.

If you're wise, you drop your tools and walk.

Slow. Never run.

They say those knocks saved lives — but not always.

Not if you ignored them.

Not if they meant you.

Playful or Punishing

Some claim the Knockers are tricksters—crawling things with long arms and sharp, laughing teeth.

They steal lunches.

Turn off headlamps.

Drop stones on your boots just to hear you curse.

But it's not fun they're after.

It's attention.

It's obedience.

Miners learned to leave a slice of bread or cake stuck in the shaft wall before their shift. A gift. A bribe. Or maybe just a way to say: "We know you're here."

The Day They Rest

Weekdays, the knocks may come. But on Saturdays—nothing. That's the day the Deep Folk sleep, or so they say.

But it's also when most cave-ins happen.

With no knock.

No sound.

Just the earth swallowing the light.

Miners began calling Saturdays "the blind day."

Because even if your eyes were open, the mountain didn't see you anymore.

What They Look Like (If You See Them)

Not many live to tell it.

But one man a cutter from the Buffalo Ridge shaft—swore he saw one just beyond the edge of his lamplight.

Said it was long and slick, naked as bone, its skin the color of old tallow—wet and twitching, with blue veins pulsing across its back like tree roots crawling under ice.

It was pressed against the wall—not standing, not crouching, but blending, like a sickness born in the stone.

Its fingers were too many.

Each ended in a nail like a fish hook.

And it whispered. Not to him. To the coal.

He dropped his pick and never came back.

Another miner — after crawling free from a collapsed shaft in '36 — said this before leaving for good: "You don't ask why the knocks come. You just say thank you… and walk out slow."

The Mirror
(Mason County)

"Cover the glass when someone dies—
Or she'll step out with hollow eyes."

There Was Once an Old Boarding House

Along the crooked backroads of Mason County, not far from the gray stretch of the Ohio River, stood a place locals would not name after dark.

They just called it the Cranley House. In the early 20th century, a woman named Eloise Cranley arrived from Louisiana—tall, pale, and always in black.

49

Her French Acadian roots marked her as strange to the townsfolk. But it wasn't her accent that kept people away.

It was what she brought with her.

A mirror.

Not just any mirror—an heirloom, she claimed. One passed down through generations of women in her bloodline. It hung in the upstairs room of her boarding house like a window someone forgot to close.

The Room Where You Don't Look Too Long

Those who rented the upstairs room didn't stay long. They complained that the mirror moved when they didn't.

That their reflections smiled on their own.

That the room was always cold, even in August.

And that, sometimes, the mirror didn't show their face at all — but someone else's.

Old.

Withered.

Dead-eyed.

Some swore they saw things behind them in the glass—events that hadn't happened yet or couldn't.

One woman ran screaming after seeing herself clawing at her own throat.

Another was found at sunrise sitting cross-legged in front of it, muttering, her eyes rolled white.

The Woman and the Mirror

Miss Cranley warned her boarders never to speak in front of the mirror. Never to sleep facing it.

Never to leave it uncovered when someone had just died. She claimed the glass held "thin skin"—that it let things through.

And if you weren't careful, "it might let something stay."

When she passed, no priest came. No family arrived.

She died upstairs, in that room, with the mirror uncovered.

What's Left Behind

The house rotted. The porch caved in. Ivy crept across the walls like veins on a corpse.

Teenagers who dared each other to sneak inside the abandoned house never returned the same. One girl claimed the mirror rippled like water when she approached.

Another said she saw Miss Cranley behind her — mouth moving, eyes black and wet.

But no sound came out. Just a slow breath on the glass.

But the mirror never cracked.

And it never collected dust.

When the Cranley Boarding House was torn down, someone—no one quite remembers who—took the mirror.

No one knows where it is now. Not for certain.

But mirrors have a way of turning up. In attic corners.

Estate sales. Quiet little antique shops where the lights flicker just so.

Maybe you'll find it.

Maybe you already have.

Bring it home.

Hang it where the moonlight touches it just right.

And wait.

You might hear her first—the breath behind the glass.

Or catch the faint sound of skirts brushing floorboards.

Because if the mirror has found you,

Miss Cranley won't be far behind.

She never liked being left alone.

Phantom Miner of Tug Fork
(Mingo County)

"Follow not the lantern's gleam, or you'll wake inside a dead miner's dream."

Where Blood Fed the Water

The Tug Fork River slithers like a vein carved deep into the flesh of Mingo County—bleeding along the border of Kentucky, trailing through Wayne, whispering to the black mud of coal country. It winds through ruin and history for nearly ninety miles, its waters thick with the memory of violence. Not just the Hatfields and McCoys.

Not just the blood feud that painted its banks red.

But the mines. The men who died in them.

The ground was never safe. Shafts collapsed like lungs caving in. Fires roared underground with no warning. The air itself could choke you. And when the strikes came—the Matewan Massacre on May 19, 1920—men died with their eyes open. Detective corpses lay face-down in the street. Ten dead. Sid Hatfield emptied his revolver at Baldwin-Felts agents who were tossing miners from their homes like trash.

And yet, that wasn't the worst of it.

A Lantern That Burns Without Flame

They say there's a light along the Tug Fork. A dim, unnatural flicker just out of reach. Some think it's swamp gas. Others know better.

He was a miner—no one remembers his name now, just the light he left behind. Trapped after a cave-in, maybe, or buried alive when a vein exploded. There was no rescue. No funeral. Just the long silence that follows the sound of breaking rock. And then the lantern appeared.

No flame. No smoke. Just a swaying glow moving through the trees at night, along the riverbanks near Matewan, Kermit, and the black hollows where old shafts still breathe foul air.

And if you follow it, God help you.

The Ones Who Come Back *Wrong*

Some have chased the light, thinking it was a hiker, or a child, or a trick of the fog.

They say the Lantern Man doesn't speak, doesn't stop. You only hear digging. Wet, scraping, hopeless digging—like bone on stone. Sometimes whispers. Sometimes crying.

A fisherman saw it near the river's bend. They found him two days later, lying in the shallows with water in his lungs and coal dust packed under his nails. A young couple driving near the Dingess Tunnel swerved off the road, trying to follow the light. When they were pulled from the wreck, both were alive—barely. But they wouldn't speak. Wouldn't blink. Just stared, soaked and shivering, at something no one else could see.

Some say those who follow the Lantern Man get taken underground. Not all the way dead, just... lost.

Stuck between.

Because the light doesn't want help. It wants to be followed. It wants company. And if you wander too long down those banks, it'll find you. It'll show you where the ground never stopped breathing.

Where the coal still sings for blood.

And when they pull you out, if they do, you'll be changed.

You'll come back damp. And quiet.

And maybe, just maybe, you'll carry a lantern too.

The Cabin that Wept Blood
(Greenbrier County)

"Rain runs red where the floorboards rot,
She screams through wood, though breath she's not.
The walls remember, the hearth still weeps—
For murder wakes what never sleeps."

Where the Rain Runs Red

Deep in the broken folds of Greenbrier County, where the mountains sink into themselves, and the trees crowd close like mourners at a grave, there was a cabin no one claimed.

It stood at the end of a deer path, crooked and leaning, half-swallowed by brush and memory.

The locals said it used to belong to a man and his wife—though no one remembered their names. They were quiet, kept to themselves, and took no visitors. Then, one day, they were simply gone.

Years later, a traveler strayed off course during a late October storm. The map had smeared in the rain, and he found himself stumbling into a hollow where the trees opened like jaws, and the wind died. That's where he saw it: the cabin. Still standing. Still waiting.

The door creaked open on its own. Inside, it was stale with rot and old smoke.

One plate.

One spoon.

A rusted fork set beside a cold bowl of congealed stew still on the stove. Ash in the hearth. A pair of boots by the bed. It looked like whoever lived there had just stepped out... years ago.

He should have left then.

But the rain was picking up, a needling mist turning to a sheet. So he stirred the coals, laid a few damp logs on the fire, and made camp for the night. That's when he noticed it.

A stain. Black and brown and too wide to be a spill. It seeped up through the wooden planks, spreading slow like something was still bleeding beneath. He stepped around it, convinced it was old stew or mold—or worse, a dead possum—but told himself not to look too close.

The Roof That Wept

That night, the rain grew angry. Wind howled through the chimney. Branches scraped the roof like fingernails on a coffin lid. Around midnight, he heard dripping. Not just from the corners or gutters—inside. He lit a stub of a candle, pulled some pans from the kitchen, and placed them under the worst of the leaks.

And that's when he saw it.

The water pooling in the pots wasn't clear. It was red. Murky and thick as syrup. He leaned closer. The smell hit him then—iron and rot, like butcher's runoff. The ceiling groaned. Something above shifted.

He ran.

He didn't gather his things. Didn't look back. He just fled, slipping through the woods like a hunted thing until the trees spat him out on the edge of town by sunrise.

The Story the Town Remembered

At a boarding house, he tried to make sense of what he'd seen. But the keeper, an old woman with tobacco-stained fingers and milky eyes, didn't blink.

"Oh, you went up there," she said. "Should've known by the stink."

She poured him coffee and told him the rest.

Years ago, the man who built that cabin lived quietly with his wife. No one knows what turned him. Rage, drink, madness, the Devil. One night, he killed her— strangled her, some say. Others claim he crushed her skull with a fire poker. He dragged her body beneath the floor and buried her under the hearthstone.

It didn't take long before the blood came back.

First, a stain in the corner. Then it spread. Through wood. Through stone. It oozed up during storms. Dripped from the eaves like tears from the boards themselves.

Curious men went up to see it. One pried up the planks. They found her.

Half-mummified. Flesh like jelly clinging to bone. Her hair still tangled around the stone that crushed her. And worst of all—her mouth. Still open. Like she'd been screaming for years beneath the floor.

They buried her in a shallow grave just outside the cabin.

But it didn't matter.

The blood kept coming.

The Curse That Soaked the Soil

No amount of scrubbing helped. New planks warped and turned dark. New roof shingles still wept. People claimed to hear crying from beneath the floorboards. Soft dragging sounds in the night. Some said they saw a pale face staring out from the cracks when lightning lit the windows.

Animals wouldn't go near it. Dogs growled at the wind if it blew from that direction. Crows perched on its roof and never cawed.

Children dared each other to run up and touch the doorknob.

Some did.

One boy came back white-haired by dusk.

One girl said something whispered through the keyhole, begging her to "come down and finish what was started."

Nobody stayed in that cabin long.

And even now, when the rain is just right—warm and red-tinted like something draining from a wound—you might see the old roof again through the trees.

And if you get too close, the air will taste of rust. And something underneath your feet will shift.

Because she's still there.

And the cabin still bleeds.

The Hollow-Eyed Watcher of Dead Man's Curve
(Raleigh County)

"He waits where the twisted headlights gleam,
Where wheels go silent and drivers scream."

Where the Road Bends and the Dead Wait

Birchton is a ghost of a coal town—nothing left but sagging bones and black dust. The coal companies stripped it bare, then vanished like buzzards after the meat was gone. Rusted train tracks. Sagging porches.

Thick hills hemming it in like a grave dug too tight. Route 3 snakes through it, tracing the old railbed like it's still looking for something it lost.

And then there's the curve.

Birchton Curve. Folks don't call it that, though—not anymore. They call it Dead Man's Curve. Sharp as a scythe. Blind as a coffin. More than a dozen people have died there over the years—cars wrapped around trees, trucks flipped in ditches, bodies pulled from crushed metal in the dark.

But it's not just the shape of the road that kills.

The Man with No Eyes

They say something waits there.

Not a ghost. Not quite.

He stands just off the shoulder. You don't see him at first—only the shape, tall and still, like someone waiting for a ride that'll never come. He doesn't wave. Doesn't move. Just watches.

His face is the part people remember. Or try to forget.

He has no eyes. Just black hollows, deep and wide, like something scooped out his soul and left the holes behind. He doesn't blink. Doesn't breathe. Just stares.

And if you flash your lights at him... if you mistake him for a stranded man... the next turn is yours to take alone. Because they say that once you see the Hollow-Eyed Watcher, your brakes stop working. Your headlights go dim. The wheel won't answer you anymore. And the last thing you'll see in the mirror is him—still standing—closer now. Smiling.

Don't Stop. Don't Look. Don't Flash Your Lights.

One man claimed he hit the figure. Swore it stood in the center of the road. Said the body crumpled like paper under his bumper, but when he stepped out, there was nothing. No blood. No body. Just hollow tracks in the gravel leading back toward the woods—and a single handprint burned into the windshield glass from the inside.

Another driver said the figure was already there after the crash. Watching from the ditch as they pulled her brother out with a broken neck. Just standing there. Unblinking. As if waiting to see who lived and who didn't.

Locals say he only appears for the dead. Or the ones marked for it.

If you find yourself on Route 3 late at night, and the curve comes too fast, don't look to the side of the road. Don't flash your lights. Don't slow down. Drive steady. Eyes forward.

Because if you do see him—just once—you'll understand what those hollow eyes are really looking for. But it will be too late.

The Coal Witch of Cabin Creek
(Kanawha Valley)

"She sings where no song ought to be, With blood on her lids so she can see. If stone should crack or tunnels groan, She's seen your name carved into bone."

Born in Blood, Bound to the Black

Cabin Creek begins in the broken hills of western Fayette County. But no one calls it gentle. Not here. It cuts through the land like something angry, winding past slag heaps, rusted rail ties, and hollow-eyed company towns before vomiting into the Kanawha River.

They say it was cursed from the start.

In the 1740s, Patrick Flynn built a cabin beside that creek—thick timbers, stone hearth, a place to raise his family in the wild. But the land didn't want them. One night, Native raiders fell upon the homestead. They took two of the children. The rest they slaughtered. The cabin burned so hot it turned the stone red.

The creek has been named for that ruin ever since.

And some say the earth never forgot.

The Mine as Mouth, the Hills as Tomb

A century passed, and coal was ripped from the veins of Cabin Creek like marrow from a dying beast. The hills groaned. The water turned black. Men sweated and bled in the tunnels while the company men grew fat.

Then came 1912. The strikes. The gun thugs. The hunger. The blood. Miners buried alive in collapses. Men were shot in the streets for speaking up. Children with coal-dust lungs gasping before they'd turned ten. It was hell, and the land watched it all.

And from that hell, something began to whisper.

They called her the Coal Witch.

She Who Sees in the Dark

No one knew where she came from. She wasn't young. Wasn't old. Just there—wrapped in rags and soot, bird bones strung around her neck, eyes like wet coal. They say she smeared sparrow blood on her eyelids so she could see through stone. Not superstition. Not a joke. She knew when the roof would fall.

When the gas would ignite.

When the boss's boot would come down.

Miners feared her. Miners followed her.

If she came to the shaft mouth and nodded, the men walked away. If they didn't, the names went up on the blackboard before sundown.

One man said she sang to him. Said her voice came from inside the wall—deep in the seam, behind the pick-scarred rock. Said he dropped his lamp when he heard her. Said the coal was singing, moaning, like it wanted him dead. And maybe it did.

The next day, that section collapsed. Killed four. He never went back.

Protector. Harbinger. Punisher.

Some said she was a spirit of the land. Some said she was the ghost of one of Flynn's daughters, dragged into the hills and fed to the roots. Others said she was the land—what little good was left of it, buried alive but still fighting.

She warned. She cursed. She chose.

One foreman who mocked her spit blood for seven nights and drowned in it. Another tried to burn her out of her hovel—he was later found in a mine cart, eyes gone, mouth packed with raw coal, jaw snapped like a hinge.

But she wasn't always cruel. A woman said the witch knocked at her door one night, muttering about her husband. Told her not to let him go down the number five shaft the next morning. The woman begged him to stay. He did. That shaft exploded before lunch.

The Creek Still Remembers

Today, Cabin Creek runs quiet again. Most of the mines are sealed. The strikes are history. The towns are rotting.

But sometimes, the water smells like blood.

Sometimes, the wind hisses down the old shaft mouths.

And sometimes, a child playing by the river will bring home a small, old bone on a string—too clean, too smooth, still red at the ends.

And they say if you hold it close and press your ear to the coal...you might still hear her singing.

The Baby That Was Never Born
(McDowell County)

"It never breathed, it never fed—
Still something cries beneath the bed.
No name, no face, no lullaby—
Just tiny nails that scratch and try."

Where the Grave Breathes

In the hills behind Wilcoe, where the trees grow too close, and the paths vanish if you blink, there once stood a one-room cabin—slumped at the edge of a ravine like it was trying to fall in.

They say a woman lived there, swollen with child and alone but for the coal dust clinging to her windows. Her husband had gone to the mines that morning. She sent for the midwife early, knowing the baby would come fast. But the woman never made it. Lost in the fog. Some say the horse refused the trail. Some say she turned back when she saw a figure walking beside her that left no prints.

By the time help arrived, it was too late.

They said the baby was stillborn. But no one saw the body. Just a blood-slick cloth and a mother staring into the hearth like it had spoken to her.

That should've been the end of it.

But the crying started that night.

What Cries From the Ground

It wasn't the wind. It wasn't a fox. It came from beneath the house—thin and wet, like lungs that didn't work right. The mother swore she heard it scratching under the floorboards. She'd rock and hum and whisper "hush now" to something no one else could see.

Neighbors came by and left shaken. The rocking chair moved when no one sat in it. The crib—still empty—would sway as if rocked by small, unseen hands.

A cloth diaper was found folded at the foot of the bed, soaked through with something dark and sticky.

They say the crying echoed all through the holler for weeks. No one would walk the trail after sunset.

No dogs would go near the cabin.

And then the grave appeared.

The Grave With No Name

A small plot on the ridge behind the house. Unmarked. No stone. Just a hump in the earth with a little wooden cross tied with twine and bird feathers. And every spring, it would sink—as if the earth exhaled—and swell again before the first thunderstorm.

One day, a boy wandered too close and found a rattle half-buried in the dirt. Made of bone. Threaded with hair. Hollowed out and filled with tiny pebbles that clicked like teeth when it shook.

He brought it home.

That night, he screamed so loud his father buried the thing in the stove and let it burn to ash. The crying came back the next rain.

It Was Never Buried Right

Old folks say the baby never took a breath—but something else did. Something small and cold that curled around its bones and never left. Maybe it wasn't born of woman but of the land. Of grief. Of rot. Something that should've stayed in the dark.

And if you go out after a storm and listen real close… you might hear it crying again.

Not loud. Just enough to make you turn.

And if you follow the sound, you might find the grave.

But you won't find your way back.

The Bride in the Fruit Cellar
(Mason County)

"She went for apples, soft and red—
She came back silence, came back dead.
A mouth of peels, a clawed-up floor—
Now she waits behind the cellar door."

The Bride Who Vanished

In the Mason County hills, where the fog clings like cobwebs and the soil remembers every footstep, there stood a homestead with a root cellar carved into the earth—stone-walled, damp, and cold, even in July.

A man brought his new bride there. She was young, quiet, with eyes like river glass. The neighbors said she never smiled but kept the house clean and the garden neat. One autumn evening, she went down into the root cellar to fetch apples for a pie.

She never came back.

The man claimed she ran off. Said she was unhappy. But folks whispered. They'd heard screams that night—muffled like someone trying to cry out with a mouth full of dirt.

The Cellar That Weeps

Weeks later, a curious and uneasy neighbor ventured into the cellar. The air was thick and heavy with rot. On the floor lay apple peels—fresh, though no apples had been picked in days. And in the corner, a patch of earth was disturbed, as if something had been hastily buried.

They dug.

Beneath the soil, they found her. Fingernails torn, mouth stuffed with apple peels, eyes wide open, staring into the dark. She had tried to claw her way out.

They gave her a proper burial. Sealed the cellar. But the house was never the same.

The Ghost That Waits

After dusk, the air around the cellar grew colder. The door would creak open on its own.

Visitors heard whispers—soft, pleading. Some saw a pale figure peeling apples with fingers worn to the bone in the garden.

Children dared each other to touch the cellar door.

Those who did often fell ill—fevers, nightmares, a lingering sense of being watched.

No one stayed in the house for long.

Tenants came and went, each leaving with stories of the woman who never left, of the root cellar that refused to forget.

The Curse That Lingers

They say the land remembers. That her spirit clings to the place where her life was stolen. The root cellar is a wound in the earth that will never heal.

And if you find yourself near that old homestead, and you hear the soft sound of peeling or catch the scent of fresh apples in the dead of winter, turn away.

Do not open the cellar door.

Some things are meant to stay buried.

The Hound and the Grave
(Clay County)

The Eccentric Prophet

Robert Sheffey was a strange man. Thin, soft-spoken, with eyes that always looked a little too far behind your shoulder. He mumbled when he tried to preach, fumbling scripture like a drunk with matches. But when he prayed—really prayed—the ground listened. They say he rode 14 counties as a circuit preacher, more ghost than man, arriving on foot or mule with nothing but his Bible, a woolen shawl, and strange stories trailing behind him. He'd sleep in barns. Whisper to animals.

Spend nights on hillsides shouting at the moon.

And he hated liquor like it was the Devil's spit.

The Prayers That Destroyed

One summer, Sheffey visited a mining camp near a sluggish creek lined with distilleries. He was welcomed with mockery. The men there drank hard and worked harder. But Sheffey wasn't interested in converting their hearts—he wanted their stills turned to ash.

He stood knee-deep in the creek and prayed, long into the night, for their destruction.

The first owner—healthy, red-faced, proud—was found the next morning in his bed, blue-lipped and cold. The coroner said apoplexy.

Others said he heard Sheffey whispering through the wall just before he died.

The second distillery? There wasn't a tree within thirty yards. Still, Sheffey said, "May God bring it down." That night, a lightning storm blew in.

The sky cracked open and something—oak, pine, no one could say—smashed the roof in with such force the stone furnace split like a skull.

The third burned.

Sheffey had spent the evening pacing outside it, muttering into the dark.

By dawn, it was blackened rubble, the air reeking of scorched mash and scorched meat.

No one laughed at his prayers after that.

Some men packed up and left without a word, afraid they'd be named next.

The Hound and the Grave

Sheffey died in 1902 and was buried at Wesley Chapel Cemetery near White Gate. The grave was plain. Just a name carved into soft stone and a chill that hung around longer than the season allowed. Death didn't keep him.

Weeks later, a dog began appearing near the grave. No collar. No tracks. It would whine and dig—relentlessly—at the earth. Locals tried to chase it off. It vanished into the trees like smoke, only to return by sundown, eyes like cinders, paws soaked in mud.

One morning, they found the grave torn open.

The preacher's coffin had been pried apart. Inside, his body wasn't at rest. His hands were curled into claws, broken nails jammed with splinters and fabric. The Bible buried with him—his only request—was in shreds, the pages stuck to his ribs. One page had been chewed to a pulp and crammed into his mouth.

And there were tracks leading away from the grave. Too large for a dog. Too long for a man. They followed them until the prints just... stopped.

Was It A Dog?

Some say the creature was no dog at all, but a shadow given shape. Others believe it was the Devil who came to reclaim a man who had prayed too hard and too often, who called down curses in the Lord's name and got too good at it. Now, when preachers pass that cemetery, they do not stop. The grass doesn't grow right there. And if you visit at night and say his name three times, they say you'll hear it—the sound of breathless prayer, rising from beneath the earth. And something listening.

The Eye in the Creek
(Fayette and Nicholas County)

"Don't look down into the creeks—
An eye awaits; it watches, it seeks."

Where the Water Sees You Back

Deep in the hollers where the moss never dries, and the sun rarely makes it past tree canopy to the earth, a narrow creek carves through the shale and root-choked woods of Fayette and Nicholas Counties. It babbles like any other—until nightfall. That's when it changes. That's when it watches.

They call it the Eye in the Creek.

It doesn't blink.

It doesn't ripple.

It just stares.

The Boy Who Dove Too Deep

The old-timers tell of a boy—barefoot, grinning, dumb with summer—who dared to dive where the water ran deep and too still. The grown folk warned him: Don't go near where the water thickens. Don't stir what watches. But boys don't listen.

He jumped.

And the creek swallowed him.

They say he came back up screaming, hair gone white like chalk dust, eyes rolled so far back they saw nothing but bone. He clawed at his throat like something was still holding him.

Later, when he could speak again—if you could call it that—he described what he'd seen:

A girl.

Not swimming.

Floating.

Her skin looked wrong—bloated, slick like a bar of wet soap left out too long. Her mouth stretched open in a scream that didn't end. Worms wriggled through her gums. Her eyes—those awful, soupy eyes—were black but soft and runny, with pale rings like eggshells around the pupils.

She reached for him. Her arms were too long. And her fingers...bent backward.

The Eye That Remembers

Some say it wasn't the girl at all—it was her eye. One eye, wide and wet, still drifting in the current. On certain nights, when the water is still as glass, and the moon is too close, it rises. Just beneath the surface. Just enough to look back.

People say if you see it, you'll feel a tug.

Not on your clothes.

Not on your limbs.

But on your soul.

It wants you.

It wants you to come closer. To lean in. To slip. To sink.

To join her.

And if you do?

You don't just drown.

You rot from the inside out.

You change.

What the Water Keeps

They say the girl was never baptized. That she died wrong—alone, angry, unloved—and the creek took her in like a mother with a grudge. It clothed her in mud and bone, fed her fish, and filled her mouth with silence.

Now, she watches for another.

Someone hollow.

Someone broken.

Because no spirit likes to stay buried alone.

Wizard Clip
(Jefferson County)

"Snip-snap went the devil's shears,
Cutting clothes and feeding fears."

The Guest Who Should Not Have Died

It began in 1791 with a knock at the door. A stranger—pale, gaunt, shivering—asked Adam Livingston for a place to rest. The Livingstons, stern Protestants of German stock, let the man in, gave him bread, and showed him to a room. That night, the household stirred to soft groaning behind the door. Adam approached.

The man inside said he was dying—he begged for a priest. A Catholic priest.

Adam scoffed. His father had fled Catholic persecution in the Old Country. A priest? In this house?

When the man begged again, naming the McSherrys and Minghinnis as neighbors who might help, Adam's wife cut in from the shadows of the hall: "No Papist will set foot under this roof. Let him wait for morning."

And so he did. But the morning found him cold, stiff, dead in the bed.

The House That Would Not Stay Quiet

Adam buried the man quick, shallow, and alone. No rites. No stone. Just silence.

But the silence did not stay.

That very night, the man hired to sit vigil fled screaming.

The candles kept going out.

Shadows moved.

Something whispered from the hearth.

Then, the house began to twist.

Logs leapt from the fireplace and danced like dogs possessed.

Crockery shattered from untouched shelves. Burning coals bounced across the floor like teeth from a snapped jaw.

Invisible horses thundered through the parlor. Guests swore they saw ropes strung across the road that couldn't be cut—ropes made of air.

And then came the clipping.

Snip. Snip. Snip.

It began as a sound in the walls. Shears—snipping, snapping in rhythm.

Then shirts, dresses, boots, sheets—all torn in crescent shapes. The family opened trunks from years past and found all their stored garments shredded, precise, moon-shaped. The cuts were always fresh. Always new.

Even a foolish boy who mocked the spirit had his britches fall in tatters to his ankles before he could fire a shot.

Chickens were found dead in the yard—heads snipped clean off, bloodless.

People came to witness it. Some tucked away handkerchiefs as proof. When they returned home, they unfolded their cloth to find it cut. Always the same shape.

One night, ducks were beheaded mid-step in front of a crowd.

No Holy Words in This House

Livingston tried conjurers. Snake-oil men. Herbalists. One gave him a riddle, herbs, and a book. He tucked them into a chamber pot.

The ghost laughed.

The shears grew bolder. Furniture flew. Shadows screamed. The smell of rot poured from the hearth.

Then Adam dreamed—a burning dream. He climbed a snarled hill, roots wrapping his feet. At the top stood a man in long robes, backlit by fire.

"This is the one who will free you," the voice said.

The Last Cut

Desperate, Adam swallowed pride and sought the Catholic neighbors—the very ones he'd mocked. They led him to a priest. When Adam saw him, he wept—the same robed man from his dream.

The priest blessed the house. The shears quieted. But not for long.

It took a full Mass to silence it.

A final rite.

The clippings stopped when Father Cahill of Shepherdstown celebrated Mass on the haunted floorboards.

The shadows fled. The house finally slept.

Adam, trembling, converted. He gave 35 acres of his land to the Church.

When he left West Virginia in 1802, the hauntings were over. But for years, the house stood empty. No one would cut timber from that land.

Even now, the woods grow twisted near Middleway.

And sometimes, if the wind blows just right, you can hear it.

Snip.

Snip.

Snip.

Thump-Thump at Falling Run
(Monongalia County)

"Before the books, before the bell,
The black creek ran through hill and dell.
A hanging tree with roots like claws—
It birthed a wraith that snaps and gnaws."

Morgantown's Dark Secret

Before it was West Virginia University, the land it lays upon had a creek with a tree. Before stadiums and sidewalks, *that* black creek cut through the valley— Falling Run, they called it.

It murmured through woods and stone, winding past moss-slick banks and a waterfall that spilled white and cold from a jagged cliff.

And there stood *that* tree.

It rose as thick as a stone chimney, with roots like gnarled arms reaching into the soil and boulders alike. It was old—older than the town, older than the graves, older than the church bells. It was almost as if it had a mind of its own. It was a living thing that could not stop being forced to hold the rope in one arm that was used to dispose of the bad, the evil, the wrong-doers. It offered its limbs, like it or not. *The hanging tree.* And in the summer of 1827, another rope was suspended on its tree limb.

Joshua was eighteen. A slave owned by James Collins. He was tried and convicted, quickly and publicly, for a woman's brutal assault. They didn't wait long to kill him. A rope was slung over the biggest limb of the great tree by the creek.

A noose knotted tight.

He sat in the buckboard wagon beneath the swaying rope, staring at it—not blinking.

"I'm not afraid of dying," he said, voice low. "But what's to become of my body after I'm dead?"

A preacher mumbled something about his soul, his father, forgiveness. But the mob wasn't listening.

They kicked the wagon.

The rope snapped taut.

And then—it broke.

Not the rope. Him.

Thump. His feet struck the earth.

Thump. His head followed—snapped clean. Those standing closest vomited. Some heard the tree groan as if it had swallowed something it didn't want.

They buried Joshua—or what was left of him—somewhere shallow and silent. Maybe his father came for him. Maybe not. But the tree kept the rest.

The Valley Doesn't Sleep

For years after and even when they built the Sunnyside Bridge crossing the valley, folks walking near the tree at dusk heard rustling—something twisting mid-air.

Then, a heavy, deep sound: *Thump. Thump.*

They saw nothing. But the whisper came anyway, curling close to the ear like a worm: "I'm not afraid of dying... but what's to become of my body after I'm dead?"

People stopped using that trail. Those who crossed the Sunnyside Bridge said they could see something writhing near the tree—a shape hanging, thrashing like it still hadn't finished dying. Then it would drop.

Thump. Thump.

And follow.

Buried Again

In the 1920s, progress came swinging. The university cut the valley open with knives of concrete and pipe.

So they did not have to be reminded, they chopped down the same old tree they made a hangman, though its limbs never asked to bear the dead.

Diverted the creek.

Paved over the roots with a football field—
Mountaineer Field—built atop the corpse of Falling Run.

The water was silenced.

The tree was forgotten.

And for a time… it was quiet.

But Nothing Stays Buried

They tore the stadium down in the late 1980s. What was hidden rose again. The land was bare for the first time in decades. The ghosts could stretch their limbs.

And people began to see a shape again—underneath the soft lawn below Woodburn Hall.

A shadow hung where no tree stood. It writhed, twisted in the air. And then:

Thump. Thump.

Some thought it was footsteps. Some thought it was a body.

Those who walked the path late, alone, near midnight, said they heard the whisper—so close it felt warm: "I'm not afraid of dying… but what's to become of my body after I'm dead?"

The answer was the same as ever: buried, burned, or forgotten.

But not forgiven.

And never at peace.

He still hangs.

He makes sure that those who pass by will not ignore him. And perhaps he has worse intentions in mind.

The Witch Ball
(Roane County)

*"She reached through flame to pay her debt,
and vanished ere the sun had set."*

The Boy was Rotting

The boy was decaying before their eyes.

Gaunt. Colorless. His skin was like melted wax. His lips flushed the pink of dried blood, and his breath rattled like a stovepipe in the wind. Black rings grew under his eyes like bruises left by unseen fingers. By week's end, he couldn't speak. He just lay there—watching the ceiling.

Or maybe something above it.

The doctor called it consumption. "Nothing to be done," he said, packing up his bag with shaking hands. But the old grandmother spat on the floor behind him. She knew better.

His grandmother, wrinkled as bark and bent from years, never trusted town doctors. She'd seen this before. This was no illness. Something had him. Something dark. Something feeding. Something was stealing him. Bit by bit. And it wasn't a sickness. It was a summoning.

The Witch Ball

She sat beside him that night as his chest rose like a dying bellow and raked her mind until it bled—pulling up half-remembered whispers from her girlhood. The old stories. The protections.

Then she went to work.

She wound red thread until her knuckles cracked. She stuffed the yarn with splinters of bent silver forks, filings scraped from an old wedding band, and crushed henbane she kept for rats. She bound it all together tight—tight enough to choke a curse—and spat into it, once, for sealing.

Then she packed bread into a threadbare sack and stepped out into the dark.

The Bridge That Wasn't Built by Man

She walked alone under a slit moon to a hanging rock—an ancient, moss-cloaked bridge of stone where water carved its way through the bones of the earth. No road ran there. Only a deer path, thick with briar and silence.

They said the bridge wasn't made by man's hand. That the stream beneath it had teeth. That witches once came here to whisper.

When she reached it, the wind stank like hot iron, and her knees buckled. But she stood over the lip of the chasm, raised the witch ball high—and hurled it into the black water.

The splash hissed like steam.

She didn't look back. She walked home fast and didn't eat the bread.

Burned Hands

She returned before the rooster crowed. The boy still breathed—barely—but the room felt colder, clearer.

Morning broke. Pale and strange.

The boy still slept, but his cheeks were flushed now—alive again. His breath no longer wheezed.

Something had passed!

But there came a knock.

At the door stood a woman in rags. Her hair was wild and full of briars, and her hands—God, her hands—were blackened, blistered, and curling like old leaves. The skin hung from her knuckles in ribbons. She didn't speak, only held them out, palms up, like she was offering them—or asking forgiveness.

The grandmother screamed.

The woman turned, walked into the woods behind the house, and was never seen again.

That night, the boy opened his eyes and whispered, "It was under my bed. But it's gone now."

The Hand Behind the Door
(Wyoming County)

"Knock once, knock slow—
he paid in bone, but still he owes."

The Widow's Cabin

In the hollers of Wyoming County, where fog clings low, and winter comes cruel, there sat a crooked cabin with moss on its roof and rot in its bones. A widow lived there—sharp-tongued, bone-thin, and half-blind in one eye.

She let out rooms to poor folk, drifters and peddlers.

They were the kind who carried their lives in sacks and sold rusted knives and combs from split-lid crates.

One peddler, a man with a silver tooth and a wheezy laugh, came through often. He brought her trinkets, mirrors, and brass buttons. Sometimes, he paid for his room in coin, sometimes in trade. Sometimes, he promised to pay next time—and sometimes, she let him. But their bargains soured. Neighbors said they bickered in the dark over debts and broken promises.

The Knocking in the Snow

One morning, he was just gone. Vanished like fog off the ridge.

The widow said he left in the night. Said he took her kindness and gave nothing in return. Said she was glad to be rid of him.

But no one ever saw him again.

Then, the knocking began.

Years later, a family moved in. Snow was thick on the ground, moonlight silvering the holler. At night, something knocked at the back door—steady, patient. But there were no tracks in the snow. Nothing but the sound.

Then, the bedroom doorknob turned.

They saw it with their own eyes—a hand creeping the door open. Just a hand. No arm, no body. Blackened like burnt meat, the fingers curled and shaking, melted skin fused to the bone. The mother screamed. The hand vanished before it opened the door.

They left that night with what they could carry.

The Hearth Beneath

No one stayed long after that. The house sat empty. Until years later, a man with no fear came to gut the place. He tore up an old hearth that had not been used in a long, long time to install a new fireplace—and there they were. Bones. Cracked and scorched, curled like something buried too hot and too fast. Among them: a belt buckle with the peddler's initials, half-melted and rusted through.

Still Owed

They say the knocking still comes some winters. And if you sleep too close to the door, you'll hear the knob turn. And you might see that hand. Still trying to settle a debt no one remembers... but the dead.

Lantern Man of Long Fork
(Pike County, Kentucky and Mingo County, West Virginia)

*"He brings the light to open graves—
don't look back at the one he saves."*

Long Fork in Kentucky is a tributary of Tug Fork, which cuts a winding line along the border between West Virginia and Kentucky. As these two states share the same river, so too did the coal camps and mountain communities that rose along its banks. Miners traveled for work, families married across state lines, and their stories—dark, old, and full of dread moved just as easily.

One tale that echoed in both hollers was of the Lantern Man, a pale light that came not to guide but to gather.

The Light That Waits

They said he rose with the storms.

When the black sky dropped low, and the wind turned bitter, a lantern would bob into sight—floating where no man could stand. Too high on the ridge. Too deep in the swamp. The flame was wrong. Thin and cold, like bone-fire. It moved with a mind of its own, pausing at windows and mine mouths as if watching. Some saw a shape behind it—tall and crooked. Others said there was no shape, just the light... and the smell of wet soil.

The Boy Who Followed

In 1911, a boy in the Long Fork camp saw the light hovering beyond his yard. He thought it was his uncle, a miner overdue from a night shift. He followed the glow into the trees.

They found his body days later in a tangle of brush, face-down in the creek. His legs were broken backward. His hands were torn with claw marks—his own. His mouth had split at the corners, stretched as if something had gripped his jaw and pulled. There was no blood in his chest. Not a drop. Just bruised ribs and dirt in his lungs.

The Preacher's Price

A week later, the light came again. This time, it floated outside the cabin of a preacher who had refused to bury a bootlegger. Said no man who trafficked in sin should be blessed with holy words.

That night, the preacher's window burst inward.

He was found dead by dawn—his skin blackened from the inside, tongue split like a snake's, eyes pushed deep into his skull. There were lantern burns scorched into his sheets. But nothing had caught fire.

No Light for the Lost

They said the Lantern Man visits when the dead are cast off. When no prayer is spoken. When the dirt is shoveled too quick, or the body's left without light.

And if you see him—don't follow. Don't look too long.

Because he's not there to show the way.

He's there to finish what was left undone.

The Rebel Procession
(Randolph County)

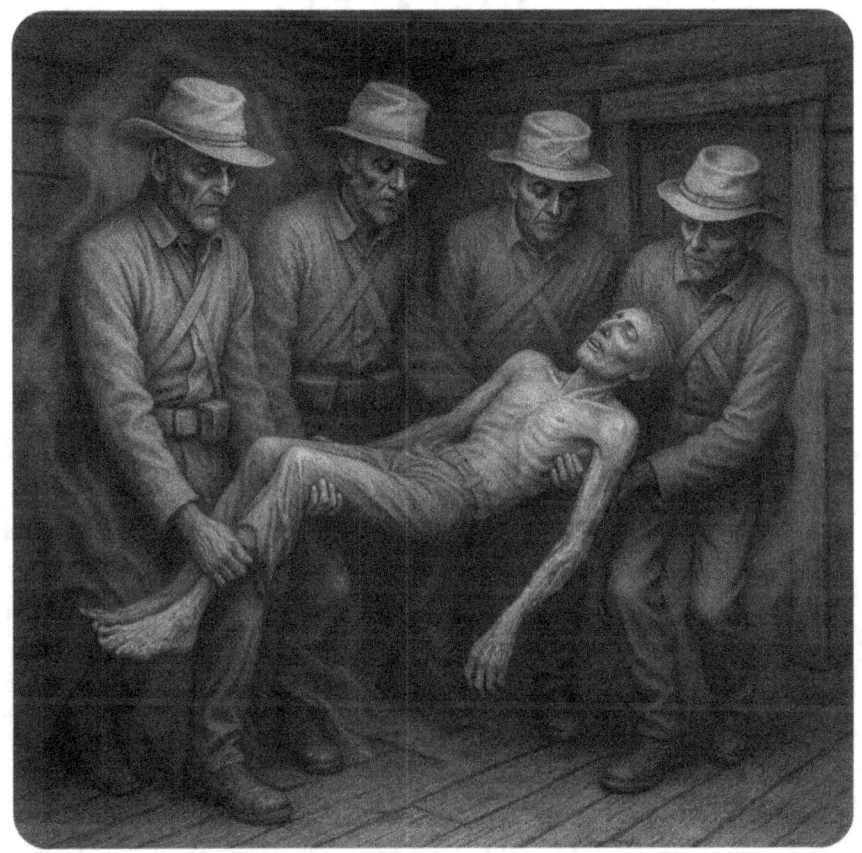

"Eight men march, the dead in tow—
he died in pain, but walks in woe."

Here Are the Rebels Again

At the war's beginning, soldiers came not just to fight but to claim the roads.

The Staunton-Parkersburg Turnpike carved through the highlands of northwestern Virginia—a pass of stone and mud, the only practical way across the northern spine of the mountains.

In the spring of 1861, Confederate General Garnett spread his men thin to protect it, posting 310 soldiers and a lone cannon at Rich Mountain.

But war doesn't wait for even numbers.

On July 11th, the rain fell in sheets as Union troops crept up the mountain. A local Union boy—David Hart, just 22—guided them along a forgotten trail behind his family's home. The Confederate camp didn't see the ambush until the fighting was on them. By 2:30 p.m., the battle was over.

Three hours of thunder.

Smoke through the trees. Blood on the ground.

One Confederate soldier was shot through in the back room of the Hart home. He died alone. The floor soaked and stained. They used the house for shelter after—torn blankets, amputated limbs, men screaming behind nailed-shut doors.

The war moved on.

But something never left that room.

The Room Where the Dead Were Never Moved

By 1867, coal miners worked the mountain's veins like ants in a carcass. Lewis Kittle, a miner from Tucker County, boarded at the Hart house with his cousin, Daniel Courtright. Neither man believed in spirits or stories. They were given the back room to sleep.

No one warned them what had happened there.

The first night, they heard knocking. Not on the walls—but under the bed. Soft. Steady. Ticking like rot peeling off the rafters. They blamed the wind.

Then came the second night. And the third.

A fellow miner pulled them aside: "Don't sleep too deep in that room. That's where the soldier went out... and he don't stay gone."

They laughed it off.

Until the night it came for them.

The Procession

Saturday. Rain again. The wind died.

Kittle lay half-asleep when the cold crept in—not the kind that chills skin, but the kind that settles in bone. The lamp flickered and then dimmed to a breath.

And then... light.

Pale and slick, leaking across the furniture, casting shadows too dark for such a weak glow.

Then came the silence. Pressed flat against the floor.

And the pull.

Not terror. Not curiosity. Just the sense that something was summoning him.

Kittle stood and walked to the door.

There, in the hallway, stood eight men.

Confederate gray. Caps in hand. Faces leached of all color—eyes sunken, some with mouths that never fully closed. They moved without sound. Four walked to the bed. Pulled the blanket. Tossed it aside like it offended them.

They bent. Lifted.

Nothing was there to see... yet their arms trembled with the weight of it. They passed the shape to the other four, who formed a solemn line.

Two marched before the dead. Two followed.

Kittle backed against the wall as they passed, and for a moment—just one—he saw what they carried.

A young soldier. Shirtless. Pale as wet ash. He wore only his trousers, boots long gone. His chest had a wound, dark and thick like it had never clotted. His eyes were closed, but his mouth hung just barely open as if he'd died trying to speak.

The door opened without a touch.

They left.

Clack. Clack.

A wooden crutch—or something worse—tapped the floor behind them.

It Doesn't Stop

Kittle returned to the bed, sweat cold on his arms. He hadn't breathed in minutes. He trembled. His mouth was dry like he had cotton balls within.

Then—again.

The lights. The weight. The silence.

But this time, they didn't lift from the mattress.

They rose the body from the floor.

They Just Keep Coming

The procession returned again.

And again.

Sometimes every week. Sometimes, multiple times in one night. Kittle and Courtright stopped trying to explain it. They would be roused from sleep—not by noise, but by something unnatural in the room's air, something that bent the night around it.

They tried moving the bed. Didn't work.

They tried speaking prayers. Didn't matter.

Eventually, they stopped fighting it.

When the pale light came and the chill set in, one of them would just whisper softly from beneath the covers:

"Here are the rebels again."

The Hart homestead is gone now. The house sagged into the earth, and the barns rotted where they stood. Nothing remains but the grass, the stones—and the silence. Only a monument endures, weathered and watching, marking the place where men bled in the yard and died in the rooms.

Travelers still come. They stand before the marker, eyes on the trees, the slope, the hush. They breathe in the stillness of the mountain, never quite sure why the air feels heavy there.

And sometimes, just as the wind shifts, the fog rolls in—thick, slow, turning like smoke through brushwood.

It coils and folds until it almost looks like men, shoulders bent, boots dragging, arms cradling a fallen shape between them.

Then it's gone.

And in the hush that follows, if you stay still—

very still—

you might hear it ride the breeze, barely above a whisper:

"Here are the rebels again."

White Bird of Death
(West Virginia)

"It perched for him, but took the man—
death flies where mercy never can."

A White Bird Flies

They say a white bird flies just ahead of death.

Not a dove. Not anything holy. It moves too slowly, its wings too wide, its eyes too human.

It doesn't cry. It watches. Perches on rooftops, fenceposts, and windowsills. And when it lands, someone inside dies.

The Bird Comes

One winter, a child took sick. The fever wouldn't break. His breathing grew shallow like the air itself had forgotten how to reach him. The house was quiet but for the sounds of boiling cloth and whispered prayers.

Then the bird came.

It perched on the eaves just before dusk, unmoving, lit by the last orange sliver of sun. Its feathers were not clean—they were pale, gray at the edges, like smoke clinging to snow.

The mother wouldn't look at it.

The grandmother wept.

The father said nothing.

That night, the bird stayed.

The Exchange

The father left after midnight. Took a lantern and walked into the woods. The snow was deep, but he didn't sink. He didn't speak. They say he walked until he found the bird again, standing on a stump, its eyes like yellow glass.

What happened next, no one knows.

The bird was gone in the morning—and the child lived. The father was found three days later, leaning against a tree in the snow, blood frozen around his mouth.

Dead. No wounds. No sign of struggle.

But the crows wouldn't go near him. And in the distance, they say the white bird flew once more—slow, heavy, circling something it had already claimed.

Headless Rider of Pleasant Hill
(Doddridge County)

*"Where the church bends low and the gravestones lean,
He rides again—silent, headless, but not unseen."*

The Place a Man was Murdered

They say *something* rides the forks of Standing Stone and Double Camp roads.

It doesn't stay in the grave where it was put. It's worst near Pleasant Hill, where the woods get too thick for comfort, and the road narrows to little more than a rut.

Where the trees breathe heavy, and the fog moves like it's remembering something, there's a lone grave just off the bend—no marker but a sag in the earth and a handful of stones gone soft with moss.

Old-timers say a traveler was killed there.

Not robbed.

Murdered.

Stabbed in the dark and buried in the ditch like a dog. The man was never claimed, and the preacher refused to bury him properly, saying a man killed on the Sabbath must've been guilty of something.

They say the body was thrown into the ground with no cloth, no coffin, and no prayer—just dirt, blood, and boots.

But the man didn't stay put.

The Weight Behind You

Long ago, when folks still traveled that road by horseback, they began to talk about a strange thing. At first, it was just a feeling—like something watching from the trees.

Then it got closer.

Riders said the horse would falter when they passed Pleasant Hill Church. A lurch. A dip in the hind legs, like an extra weight had been thrown on its back.

One man, a logger riding home at dusk, felt it for himself.

The horse buckled slightly and snorted, eyes wide. He thought it was just the old road. But then he felt it: pressure.

A heaviness. Like someone had dropped onto the back of the saddle.

He reached back to swat at what he assumed was a branch or a sack slipping loose—and his hand touched a leg.

Bare. Cold. And wrong.

Not cloth. Not leather. Not human anymore.

He turned—jerking hard—and saw a figure hunched just behind him, clinging like it meant to ride him into the next world.

It was a man or something shaped like one. Dressed in tatters. Mottled flesh, blood-stiff shirt—and no head. Just a wet neck stump, slick and black where the light hit it.

The thing didn't scream. It breathed—like wind caught in a cracked throat.

The logger jumped from his horse and ran screaming through the brush, his face scratched and bleeding from thorn and branch.

The horse bolted and was found days later, foam-drenched and shaking near a riverbank.

The Thing That Still Waits

People say you can still feel it. That if you ride or drive too slow through the curve past the church—right near that sunken patch of ground—you might hear a thump behind you. A shift in weight.

Leather creaking when it shouldn't.

Sometimes, it doesn't wait to be seen.

Sometimes, it reaches.

They say that grave was dug too shallow.

That the man was buried with his head cut off and his rage still hot.

And that every rider who passes owes him a ride— even if he has to take it by force.

So if you're ever near Pleasant Hill after dark... keep your eyes forward.

And don't, under any circumstance, look behind you.

Midnight Chain
(Calhoun County)

"Clank goes the chain at dead of night,
Down the stairs and out of sight."

A Bargain with Blood Beneath

Joe and Mary Blake never should've bought that place. Five acres of soft, black soil just outside Brooksville— going for half what land like that ought to. The house came cheap, too. They bought it from Ezra Gordon, a well-known carpenter in town. Prominent. God-fearing. Eccentric. Tight with a dollar.

Ezra's young wife had vanished not long before—rumor said she ran off with a traveling oil man. Ezra built that house for her with his hands, but the marriage soured quickly. Most folks felt bad for him... until they saw the asking price.

The Blakes moved in on a Tuesday. They cleaned every inch. Scrubbed the floors. Hung new curtains. Stocked the pantry. By dusk, they were bone-tired and asleep.

Midnight Rattling

Then the clock struck midnight.

Not just a chime—but something else. Loud. Penetrating. Shrill.

Then, a dragging noise. Metal on wood. Like a chain being hauled across the floorboards.

Mary sat bolt upright, heart hammering. "Joe," she whispered. But Joe was already out of bed, lantern in hand, checking the hall. The doors were shut. No branches brushing the roof. No animals in the yard. Nothing.

But the sound stayed with them.

The Clock Strikes and Something Follows

The next night, they were already uneasy.

At twelve sharp, the clock rang out—each chime sharper than the last. Then came the noise again. Clinking. Scraping. A heavy dragging sound just outside their door.

Mary screamed, "The chain! It's right outside—listen!"

They heard it move past their room, step by step down the hall and thudding down the stairs. Joe ran after it.

He couldn't tell if he had opened the front door himself or if it had swung open on its own. BOOM!

The night was empty. But he'd heard the chain.

He was sure of it.

The Storm Breaks the Silence

By the third night, sleep was impossible. A storm had rolled in. Thick clouds smothered the moon. Wind pressed against the glass. Thunder grumbled in the hills.

They stared at the clock. Watched each tick.

A bolt of lightning lit the room.

11:59.

Mary gripped the blankets tight. When the clock struck twelve, the chimes echoed slowly through the house—one... two... until twelve.

Then came the dragging.

Heavier now. Angrier.

The chain clattered past their door, down the hall, pounded onto the stairs, and then across the porch with a metallic slam. And then—BOOM. Something hit the ground hard, just beyond the porch steps.

Rain poured. Lightning flashed again. In the kitchen, Joe and Mary huddled, wide-eyed and silent, listening to the chain scrape over the stones in the garden.

A Grave in the Garden

When morning finally came, the rain broke. Light spilled over the soaked yard.

Mary saw it first—a dip in the earth near the hedgerow. A grave-shaped sag. Five feet long. Dry despite the storm.

Joe grabbed a shovel.

He dug. The dirt came up in thick, wet clumps. Then something dark—leather. A boot. Then, a strip of rotting blue cloth stuck to bone-white skin. A kneecap. A hand. And then the head—busted wide at the back. Her mouth was packed with mud. Her dead eyes stared skyward, glazed and filled with grit.

They had found her. Sarah Gordon.

What Ezra Buried

It all came out soon after. Sarah had hated the farm. Hated the quiet. Missed the bustle of town. The gossip. The men. She slipped away at night more than once.

Ezra didn't like that.

He chained her to the bedroom floor to keep her in. But the chain wasn't enough. One night, he split her skull with an axe. Buried her shallow in the garden she hated.

And told the town she ran off.

She Still Walks

Joe and Mary left that house as fast as they could. Others moved in after them, but no one stayed long.

The dragging chain always came back.

Always at midnight.

Same sound. Same path.

From the upstairs room, down the hall, down the stairs, across the porch, and into the garden.

Clank. Clank. Clank.

The house rotted. Weather split its boards. The town grew and eventually tore it down.

But Sarah stayed.

They say she still walks—head twisted, eyes full of dirt, dragging her chain across land that tried to forget her.

And when the wind picks up at night and the sky goes black, listen. She's still looking for someone to let her out.

Ghost of Stretchers Neck
(Mercer County)

"She waits where the tunnel cuts the stone,
rocking a child that's skin and bone."

Where the River Bends Wrong

Deep in the folds of the West Virginia mountains, where the New River cuts hard, and the rocks come up sharp, a spur of land juts out like a crooked bone. They call it Stretchers Neck. The river bends around it wide and slow, but the land itself is thin and tight, like the neck of something strangled.

Long before the trains came, before they blasted a tunnel through the spine of the mountain, there were just dirt paths, riverboats, and the black woods. It was on this neck of land, alone with her father in a cabin clinging to the ridge, that Elvira Sanner lived.

They called her "Vira." And she was beautiful in a way that made men quiet.

The Girl Everyone Wanted

Her skin was pale as milkweed sap, her lips red as dogwood berries, and her voice could hush a congregation. She wore blossoms at her throat, and the petals looked dull against her skin. Her eyes were deep and blue, like a quarry pool where light doesn't reach.

All the young men looked at her. All the old men dreamed of her. But none hungered for her like Hiram Boggass—rich, loud, and rotted with pride. He sang louder than anyone, prayed longer, and smiled wider than a man should.

And then there was Jim Thurmond—called "Chief" by the folks who knew him. He was strong and quiet, the kind of man others followed without asking why. When Elvira walked beside him, no one questioned it. Not even the men who loved her from afar.

Except for Hiram.

What Greed Buys

Hiram had land. Hiram had money. But he didn't have Elvira. And that ate at him like fly maggots on a corpse.

When Elvira's father fell on hard times, it was Hiram who offered help. Once.

Then again. Then again—until he owned the land beneath the Sanner cabin and held the old man like a dog on a leash.

Elvira's cheeks thinned. Her smiles faded.

But Jim was building a home above the bend—just beyond the rockface where the tunnel would one day run. He made apple brandy illegal but clean and sold it downstream. Everyone knew: Jim was fixing up the cabin to marry Elvira.

One day, he left for Kanawha Falls with a boatload of brandy. Hiram left, too, but no one knew where he went.

Jim came back with fine linens, carved chairs, a bed made for a bride. That night, he walked up to his still.

The officers came not long after.

The Betrayal and the Blood

They smashed the still. Beat Jim until his face ran with blood. But Jim fought back. Killed the captain. Escaped.

And when the wounded men dragged themselves to Hiram's house for shelter, Hiram ran outside and cried, "Did you get him?" Too eager. Too knowing.

Everyone saw. Everyone knew.

Jim vanished. Some said he was spotted upriver, arm bleeding, walking the tracks like a ghost himself. Some said he never made it out alive. Elvira never smiled again.

The Slow Death of Elvira Sanner

The blossoms at her neck wilted. Her skin yellowed. Her lips went pale. She wasted away. When she gave birth to her child—Hiram's child—she was already more corpse than girl.

The baby was sick from the start.

They say one night, as Elvira sat rocking the fevered child, she saw Jim. Just for a moment—standing in the shadows of the cabin. He kissed her forehead. Told her the doctor was coming. When she looked again, he was gone.

But the doctor came.

The baby lived—for a little while.

The Night They Died

When the sickness came back, Hiram rode off in the night to fetch the doctor again. He left Malviny—his sister—to stay with Elvira.

The baby died just before midnight.

Elvira sat by the fire, rocking the little body, her eyes empty. Malviny, whispering prayers, stepped outside— and saw him.

Jim.

Standing in the path. Shot through, bloodless, face half-melted in the moonlight.

She dropped to the ground before she could scream. Dead of fright.

Jim walked past her.

Inside the cabin, Elvira looked up. Her lips cracked. Her eyes glistened.

"Jim?" she whispered.

He nodded. "Hiram won't be coming back. I've come to take you and the baby home."

She stood. Put the baby in his arms. Took his hand. Smiled.

When morning came, they found her cold beside the hearth. The baby cradled in her lap.

The Tunnel Beneath the Mountain

Years later, when the railroad carved through the gorge, they blew a tunnel through Stretchers Neck—right through the place where Elvira and Jim used to meet. The tunnel became a shortcut between Prince and Quinnimont. Teachers used it. Miners used it.

But many swore they heard things in there.

Crying. Whispers.

Footsteps that didn't echo like they should.

And sometimes, just past the halfway point in the dark, a figure steps forward—tall, bloody, smiling like he remembers something awful.

And behind him—*her*.

Clutching a bundle. Eyes empty. The dogwood blossoms at her throat long turned black.

They say if you stop walking… if you listen too long… you might not come out the other side at all.

Haunting at Betts' Farm
(Calhoun County)

"It walks where wheat and sorrow grow,
an identity the afterlife refuses to show."

In the late 1800s, there was a farm three miles from Grantsville along the Little Kanawha River rumored to have a haunting.

It belonged to Collins Betts. At night, the house thumped from the inside like someone beating on the floorboards. Whispers curled up behind the walls. Doors creaked open and slammed shut when no one was near.

Some claimed Collins himself stirred the story to life with trickery—a game that soured once the fear took on a life of its own. He stopped speaking of it.

But the tale kept growing.

And what happened around the house was far worse.

The Mist Beside the Wagon

One night, Henry Stephens rode his wagon down the main road—alone but calm. He was a man who'd grown up with owls and coyotes, a man not known for fear. But on this night, something shifted.

Something wrong with the air.

The horses twitched. The wind died.

Beside the wheels, a wisp of fog floated up from the roadside... and rose. It gathered shape—man-shaped but hollow. Pale as the moon. It moved with the wagon, gliding without sound.

Stephens felt his spine crawl and his scalp prickle. He stopped the horses. Picked up stones from the road and threw them hard at the mist.

The pebbles passed through it.

It didn't blink. Didn't flinch. Just watched.

Stephens jumped back into the seat, snapped the reins, and fled into the dark, his heart punching the inside of his ribs. When he dared look back, the thing was gone. But his horses ran until they foamed at the mouth.

The Riders That Never Came

Another night, James Wolverton and his eighteen-year-old son were hauling an oxen team down the steep road above the Betts' Farm.

It was nearly midnight. The air was still.

Then, from the hollow beneath the ridge, came a deafening clatter—iron-shod hooves, sabers, shouting.

It sounded like war.

They turned just as a cavalry charge burst from the trees, ghostly and white, sabers lifted, eyes glowing like coal.

James screamed, "My God, men, don't ride over me!"

And in that breath, they were gone.

No sound. No dust. Just cold.

The Boy Who Laughed at Ghosts

There was a boy—just grown, the son of a man who swore ghosts haunted the hills. He teased his father and called him superstitious.

One night, as the boy drove the wagon alone down that same cursed road, something slipped from the brush.

It didn't walk. It glided. Death-pale and near-featureless, it floated at the horses' heads, then curved around and climbed into the wagon beside him.

He didn't move. Didn't breathe.

It turned its face to him, hollow-eyed, and whispered, "Don't be afraid."

He gasped.

Blinked.

It was gone.

The moon shone bright. The wagon was empty.

But for days after, the boy sat with his hands shaking, unable to speak a word.

Who Haunts the River Road

Some say it was the peddler, the one who vanished on the way to town—last seen with a saddlebag full of cash. His horse was found tied to a tree, swaying in the wind, but he never came back for it.

Others say it started when Old Woman Riddle died—a midwife with a black book and red string on her door.

Still others speak of the Civil War blood spilled at Sycamore Creek. On November 28, 1861, West Virginia infantrymen—barely organized, barely soldiers—clashed with ragtag Southern irregulars in a muddy bend of the woods.

Three men died. Maybe more.

No markers were left. The blood soaked into the roots.

People around Grantsville don't go near that stretch of road after sundown. They say there are too many things walking there that don't leave footprints. Horses spook. Candles blow out for no reason. And if you ride alone, sometimes... you don't stay alone.

If you hear hooves behind you—don't turn around.

If a man with no eyes offers you a ride—don't answer.

And if you see fog rolling across the river, lock your doors and light your lamps because something's come back from under the dirt, and it wants to ride beside you awhile. Or worse.

The Ghost of Gamble Run
(Wetzel/Tyler County)

"Beneath the moon on Gamble Run,
a debt remained, and justice spun."

John Gamble and his Barrel Staves

In the autumn of 1850, John Gamble was a man building a life—carpenter, farmer, river trader— anchored across the Ohio River from Sardis. He'd settled his family in a stretch of land and good timber in what would one day be called Wetzel County. His flatboat runs hauled barrel staves and tanbark to Cincinnati.

His cider press ran slow but steady in a season flush with crabapples. He was a man with calloused hands and plans for spring.

On November 12th, John Gamble loaded his skiff with empty barrels to fetch more from New Martinsville, floating them downriver through the waters of the Ohio River. But there was one stop first—the Whiteman brothers' farm. He climbed the hill by the creek to collect on a $20 note owed him for a wagon.

The brothers didn't have it. But standing in the yard that day was another man—Leban Mercer, who'd sold Gamble a calf and was owed a meager $2.

The Man with Wet Boots

Gamble offered a five-dollar bill, but Mercer had no change. The tension rose like smoke from a fire not yet seen.

Trying to ease the man's pride, Gamble confessed he had nearly $200 in his pocket and would pay the debt in full within days. He shook hands. Said his goodbyes. Walked back down the winding creek trail toward his skiff, the barrels still bobbing lightly in the water.

It was the last anyone ever saw of him.

Two days later, the skiff was found drifting, empty of its captain. The barrels still neatly stacked.

A Quiet Accusation

Rumors blackened quickly. Mercer had returned to his boarding house wet and mud-caked, though the ground had not seen rain. Soon after—without explanation—he was flashing money he hadn't earned. Money that looked a lot like Gamble's.

But there was no body. No warrant. Just whispers.

The Dead Speak at Harvest

Almost a year passed. It was November 1st, 1851. Corn husks piled high, and farmers gathered for a husking bee near Point Pleasant Ridge—a work party meant to ease the weight of harvest with laughter and flirtation.

When the last ear was shucked, and the moon had begun its slow crawl into the sky, the young men gathered for one last contest: a race to their homes by separate paths.

John Hindman, skeptical and sharp-witted, took the flat route down a shadowed hollow called Ray's Run. He moved fast. Alone.

But not for long.

The Thing in the Meadow

In a clearing, a man joined him. Quiet. Pale. Walking as if weightless beside the wagon path.

"I do believe you don't know me," the man said.

"No," Hindman replied, "can't say that I do. You from 'round here?"

"I'm John Gamble. Leban Mercer killed me. Take him up. See justice done."

The figure turned his face, half shadowed, and spoke of details never made public—how he died, what he wore, what Mercer had taken.

And then... the ghost was gone.

Hindman stood in an empty field beneath the silver light of a full moon, heart thudding against his ribs like a fist on a coffin lid.

The Trial That Wasn't Justice

At first, he told no one. He searched for signs of a prank but found none. No boot prints. No whispers. No snickers behind hands.

Eventually, Hindman broke. He described the ghost. Described the coat Gamble wore the night he vanished— details he couldn't have known.

He confronted Mercer directly and, using what the ghost told him, tricked the man into confirming details never made public.

The constables acted. Witnesses emerged: two boys had seen Gamble and Mercer walking together near the creek.

A six-foot smear in the mud was found near the riverbank.

Strands of black hair. Bits of wool cloth. A man who'd shared a room with Mercer testified that Mercer had cried out in his sleep, yelling at Gamble to let go of the money.

In Mercer's possession was the Whiteman promissory note Gamble had been carrying the night he died.

But the Law Does Not Fear Ghosts

Still… it wasn't enough.

No body. No blood. Just too many cold truths and a whisper from the grave.

The jury acquitted him.

Mercer lived out his life proclaiming innocence. But never far from a lamp. Never far from town.

He never again walked near the creek at night.

Where the Ghost Walks Still

The stream that ran beside the Whiteman place is small—narrow enough to leap across in two steps. But the old folks say it runs deeper than it looks.

They named it Gamble Run after the man who walked down it alive and came no farther. Some still say his ghost can be seen at harvest, standing near the black trees when the corn is gone, and the wind turns sharp.

Waiting.

The Ghost of Borland Springs
(Pleasants and Wood County)

*"Blood seeps deep where shadows cling;
at Borland Springs, the dead still sing."*

The Blood Never Left Borland Springs

The Borland Springs Hotel opened its doors in 1908, a grand and gleaming resort tucked into the wooded folds along Bull Creek.

Built by J.W. Grimm, it boasted sixty-five rooms, a ballroom, and a restaurant that drew guests from counties away.

The true draw, though, was the springhouse just across the road—a small, damp structure fed by cold iron-rich water. They said it healed. They said it calmed. People came to drink from it in silence, to be soothed.

August Heat

On August 16th, 1918, that quiet was shattered.

A group of women made their way to the springhouse near dusk. The day had been stifling, and the water was cool, clean. They dipped ladles. They laughed. Then the door swung open hard, and the laughter died.

John Maidens stepped in, twenty years old, full of swagger and sharp words. A few of his friends trailed behind. They shouted, jeered, kicked at benches. They sloshed the water like children and drowned the space in noise.

Frank Chandis Grimm—nineteen and hot-blooded, son of the hotel owner—heard it all from up the hill. He snatched his revolver and went running. When he entered the springhouse, he barely had time to react. A fist flew at his face. Another wound up.

Chandis fired.

Just once.

Maidens fell. The echo of the gunshot rippled through the trees. Blood ran thick and fast across the floorboards.

The Stain

It was ruled self-defense. Chandis paid a fine and walked free. But what happened inside the springhouse didn't wash away.

They tried. Sanded the floor. Painted it.

Replaced boards. But each time, the blood came back. The stain returned like something alive—growing through fresh wood, rising through coats of whitewash.

The Slow Rot

The hotel never truly recovered. Fewer guests came. By the 1950s, it was a henhouse—twelve thousand chickens clucking through the rooms where music once played. The air soured. The windows blackened.

In the 1960s, fire took what was left. Flames licked through the empty halls, and the grand structure collapsed in on itself. Only stone and ash remained.

But the springhouse survived.

The Ghost

The bully John Maidens is still walking, although he has been reduced to something far less intimidating.

He does not stop. Borland Springs grew wild, its waters clogged with weeds and decay, but the ghost remained. On certain nights, when the wind crawls through the holler and the sound of a springhouse door creaking open fills the air, passersby on the nearby road swear they see him—lurching across the expanse over the old creek heading away from the springhouse, clutching a wound that never heals, his mouth still open mid-scream.

He walks that stretch again and again, drawn back to the place his blood first soaked the wood. No matter how deep the weeds grow, or how many years pass, he does not stop. But don't get in his way. Dead or not he is a ghost of a bully who died smoldering with hate. He might still have some of that anger in him. Aimed at you.

The Tomb Where Ikie Sleeps
(Pleasants County)

"She rocked the dead in cradle's keep,
and sang him softly back to sleep."

The Tomb Where Ikie Sleeps

In the lonely hills near Algeria, there stands a tomb that no one wants to speak of after dark. It once held the corpse of a young boy. Isaac "Ikie" Mooring was just seven years and two months old when death took him. He ate ice cream contaminated with milk from cows that grazed on White Snakeroot, leading to milk poisoning.

His parents—Kenneth, an oil driller aged forty, and his young wife Emma Jane, just twenty-nine—buried him in a manner so strange, so sorrowful, that it passed into local legend with a shudder.

They placed him not in the earth but in a coffin-shaped vault inside a custom-built family mausoleum at Mount Welcome Cemetery.

It had glass windows, doors, and a casket that gleamed clear as water.

This wasn't any ordinary burial box. It was one of the new glass-sealed coffins, filled with a strong solution of alcohol meant to preserve the body in its perfect stillness.

The Mourning Mother

Emma Jane visited often. Too often, some said. She brought her boy's bicycle. His schoolbooks. Toys. She placed them carefully inside the tomb, talking softly to him as she swept dust from the floor. She'd close the glass door behind her like it was a bedroom, not a grave.

But the whispers didn't start until people began noticing stains—strange blue and white dribbles running down her dress after these visits.

When asked, Emma Jane just smiled.

Old folks still tell it: Emma Jane, crushed by grief and driven beyond reason, would unlock the coffin's seal, lift her preserved boy from the alcohol, and cradle him in a rocking chair she kept inside the tomb. She'd stroke his hair, sing lullabies, and hum to him as though he were just asleep.

And Ikie was not alone.

Three other children of Emma Jane's, also claimed young by illness, were said to rest in stone crocks inside that mausoleum. Locals said she took their bodies out as well—hung them by their collars from the tree limbs outside to let them dry in the sun.

The Crumbling Coffin

Time moved on. The family left. But Ikie stayed.

The tomb aged badly.

Its glass panels cracked. The rubber seals holding in the alcohol dissolved. The preserving liquid—Ikie's only defense against rot—evaporated.

His sailor suit yellowed.

His flesh turned dark.

Then came the vandals.

Troublemakers broke in. Animals got inside.

And one day, dogs dragged the boy's remains into the woods.

His bones were scattered under the trees until hunters found what was left. They called the authorities.

Ikie was reburied—this time in a more humble plot, outside the tomb, near his grandparents and Uncle Ralph, who died of pneumonia.

The old mausoleum remains, as do the empty spaces where the corpses and coffins laid.

Busted up, roof caved, the windows gone.

But that doesn't stop the stories.

The Crooning in the Tomb

Locals say Emma Jane never left.

Not really.

On misty mornings, or when the moon strikes the tomb just right, people have seen her.

A woman in a faded dress standing at the window, gazing inward.

Sometimes, she's inside, bent low, rocking something cradled in her arms.

Other times she sits where a long-gone bench once sat, Ikey's corpse on her lap, his sailor suit dribbling slimy something all over her shroud-like dress.

Sometimes, late at night, a lullaby hums from within the crumbling stone. Soft. Rhythmic. Loving.

And when you look through the glass, there is nothing inside.

Only the empty chair.

And the stains that never seem to wash away, just as she won't go away.

She watches now—from the window, from the trees. From the long-gone bench.

Guards the boy.

Guards the tomb.

Let the foolish laugh, but step too close, and you'll feel it—the weight of her grief, pressing cold and hard against your chest.

Because some mothers never leave.

And some graves don't forgive.

The Sodder Children Mystery
(Fayette County)

"The fire burned the walls away,
but not the eyes that watch and stay."

Burned Hollow

It was a cold and rain-slick Christmas Eve in 1945.

Jennie and George Sodder had just tucked in their youngest daughter, two-year-old Sylvia, and gone to bed themselves. Their home, a modest two-story frame house outside Fayetteville, West Virginia, pulsed with the hush of sleeping children. Ten in total.

One of the boys, Joe, was away in the Army.

The rest were nestled in rooms and hallways, the house heavy with dreams and wrapped presents waiting for dawn.

At 12:30 a.m., the telephone rang.

Jennie stirred from sleep. She picked it up. A wrong number. A woman's voice. Strange laughter. Then the line went dead.

She wandered the house afterward. Something felt off. The lights were still on. The door was unlocked. She shut things down. Turned off the lamps. Bolted the door. On the couch, nineteen-year-old Marion slept soundly.

Jennie was nearly back in bed when she heard it: a hard thud on the roof, like a heavy object tossed high. Then, a rolling noise. Then silence.

Less than an hour later, she smelled it.

Smoke.

She screamed.

Flames were already clawing up the stairwell. George scrambled up from bed. They grabbed Sylvia. They roused John, George Jr., and Marion. But Maurice, Martha Lee, Louis, Jennie, and Betty—five of them—never stirred. Not a whisper. Not a cough.

George tried to go back in.

Tried the front door. Blocked by fire.

Tried the ladder. Gone.

Tried the truck to drive it near and climb in through a window. The engine refused to turn.

The house lit up the sky.

The fire department didn't arrive until morning.

By then, the home was ash.

No bones. No teeth. No charred bodies.

Nothing.

The Lies Beneath

George was hospitalized for injuries. The town whispered. Rumors grew and transformed.

Weeks before the fire, an insurance salesman had threatened George for refusing coverage. "Your house will burn," he'd said. "And your children with it."

The Sodder boys had seen a strange man watching their younger siblings come home from school. The phone line, it turned out, had been cut—not melted.

One neighbor claimed to have seen the children peering from a vehicle that night. Another said they were spotted in Charleston. A woman swore she saw them eating breakfast with strangers.

Even worse—some say Fayetteville's fire chief admitted he found remains and buried them secretly in a dynamite box. When exhumed, the box held a raw beef liver.

Later, several vertebrae were recovered near the site, unburnt and too old to belong to a child. Forensics eventually traced them to a corpse stolen from a nearby cemetery.

What the Fire Didn't Take

George bulldozed the ruins. Left a memorial. He strung a billboard up along the highway—huge, grim, and pleading for answers. He never let go. Neither did Jennie.

She was dressed in black for the rest of her life.

They both died believing their children had not burned.

Now, a home stands where the ashes cooled. Green grass. New windows. Clean siding. Nothing that hints at the horror.

But people still talk.

They whisper about the thump on the roof.

The silence in the flames.

The five who never screamed.

Maybe they died. Perhaps they didn't.

Maybe the fire took more than bodies.

Maybe it left something behind.

Something cold that still watches from the trees.

A silence that deepens at midnight.

A presence that stirs the ashes and waits for names no one speaks aloud.

And on quiet Christmas Eves, you might still hear it when the wind presses against the windows just right. Not at the long-gone house.

But your own.

The ring of a phone. The laughter on the line. A child's whisper. A thud on the roof.

And little footsteps by your bed.

The Lantern and the Chain
(Marion County)

*"Where the chain once snapped and the blood ran black,
the brakeman's ghost still walks the track."*

The Chain

In the early 1900s, a chain clattered over the Baltimore and Ohio tracks just outside the Fairmont depot. When it rattled against the roofs of incoming railcars, it told the engineers: slow down. The depot was near. One cold night around 1915, a brakeman rode the top of a freight car, his boots gripping steel, the train hissing under him.

He turned, distracted by some noise, just as the chain swept through the air.

It struck his shoulder. Then wrapped his neck.

It took his head clean off.

The train didn't stop until it reached the depot. Workers found his body sprawled atop the car, leaking into the coal-dusted grooves. His head was a hundred feet back, lying in the gravel like something discarded.

They took the chain down.

But something else stayed.

A Ghost Walks the Tracks

Walkers on the track began to see a dim, shadowed figure swaying with a lantern in hand.

When they drew near, they saw it had no head. The body drifted along the tracks, oil-lamp flickering against the stone, until it vanished between the ties.

Some say he's looking for his head.

Others say he never knew he lost it.

But if you're walking late and alone near the empty space where the old Fairmont depot once stood, listen.

If you hear the drag of chain or the soft clink of a lantern hook, don't look behind you.

He's not far.

And he might mistake your head for his own.

Mason County Screamer
(Mason County)

"Dragged through trees and buried deep,
now Mary screams and never sleeps."

The Screams in the Big Woods

In the 1850s, David and Catherine Somerville worked a family farm near the Big Bend of the Ohio River, raising eight children on a patch of land choked with quiet trees and hills that breathed fog at dawn.

But the quiet didn't last.

Salt mining came in 1849. Then coal. Then timber.

Men by the hundreds poured in—rowdy, hungry, rough-handed strangers. And soon, the woods weren't so quiet.

One fall evening, with the family in town, nineteen-year-old Mary Somerville stayed behind. She swept the porch. Lit a lamp. Waited.

But someone else was watching.

A group of men, filthy from the mines, saw the light. Knew the house was alone. They didn't knock. They didn't ask. They broke the door.

Mary screamed.

By the time her family returned, there was blood on the walls.

Mary was gone.

They searched the hills. The brush. The banks of the Ohio. Nothing. The forest swallowed her whole.

The Crying Never Stopped

The family left the state. They couldn't stay.

But the woods didn't forget.

Lumbermen started hearing it first—long, drawn-out wails deep in the trees. It wasn't a fox. It wasn't a woman. It was something else.

The sound scraped their bones.

Then came the cops. Locals. Hikers. They'd hear screaming—like someone being killed. They'd rush into the trees. Find nothing.

And the scream would follow them back to town.

Her Grave Wasn't Enough

In 1986, during a strip-mining operation, a shallow grave was uncovered near the old Somerville property.

A skeleton, too small for an adult. Torn fabric. Scraps of bone.

It was Mary.

They moved her body to Zuspan Cemetery.

Marked her grave.

But it didn't stop.

She still screams.

Some say it's the moment they dragged her into the woods.

Some say she's calling her mother.

But if you're in the Big Woods near Hartford City, and you hear a girl crying for help—don't answer.

She isn't lost.

She was buried. And she came back screaming.

Headless Coeds of Monongalia County

(Monongalia County)

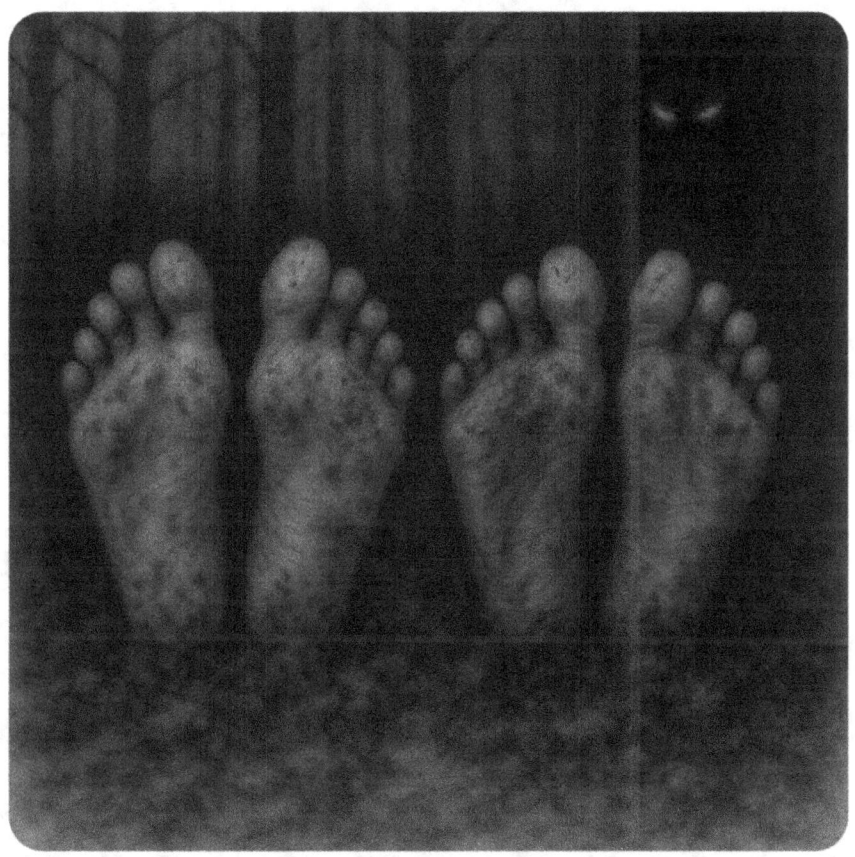

"Two girls gone where dark things tread,
now only silence speaks instead."

The Hitchhikers

In January of 1970, two West Virginia University freshmen—19-year-old Mared Malarik and 18-year-old Karen Ferrell—walked out of the Metropolitan Theatre in Morgantown after watching Oliver! and disappeared.

There were no buses, no cabs. Hitchhiking was common. They were last seen stepping into a cream-colored sedan.

They never came home.

Eighty-Eight Days

For nearly three months, the mountains swallowed the girls whole.

Flyers faded in the rain.

Hope turned rancid.

Then, on April 16, a unit of the National Guard uncovered two shallow graves near Goshen Road. The bodies were barely bodies at all—just pieces.

Decayed.

Headless.

The heads were never found.

A man named Eugene Clawson confessed. A drifter with a record and a violent past. He was convicted. But the town never bought it. Too many inconsistencies. Too few answers. And something darker lingered—just out of reach.

What They Found in the Dirt

The scene was wrong. Hasty. Unfinished. Albert "Rod" Everly, a Guardsman who helped uncover the girls, couldn't let it go. Years later, anonymous letters sent from Maryland emerged—rambling, eerie, and signed by a man claiming to receive messages from spirits. He named the place. He gave directions. And cadaver dogs confirmed it—something was beneath the soil.

Still, no heads.

Decades passed.

The woods grew back. But the road where Mared and Karen vanished? That stretch never forgot.

The Ones Without Faces

It started with drivers at dusk. A pale shape at the shoulder.

Two. No heads.

Just the sense of eyes where there were none. Some say they float. Others say they walk, hand in hand, across the blacktop.

There are stories of accidents.

Cars swerving.

Engines dying.

And always, the faint sound of crying from the tree line.

A sharp wind. And the feeling of being watched.

They call them the Headless Students of Monongalia County now.

A legend. A warning.

But the truth is worse.

There are whispers in town that someone knows.

That the killer never left.

That he walks the same streets, older now, quieter. Maybe dead—but still watching.

Some say he goes back to that road.

Stands in the trees.

Waits for the headlights.

Still watching. Still hunting.

It Happened at Lake Shawnee
(Mercer County)

"They built their joy on sacred bones,
now laughter echoes through the stones."

What the Children Found at Lake Shawnee

There are places in the world where joy leaves stains.

Lake Shawnee Amusement Park in Rock, West Virginia, is one of them. The kind of place where laughter echoes wrong. Where swings creak in the wind when the air is still. Where every ride sits rusted like a ribcage, waiting.

The First Blood

Long before ticket booths and carousels, there was blood in the soil. In 1783, Mitchell Clay carved out a farm on what was once sacred ground. The Shawnee had hunted there and buried their dead there. But settlers like Clay came with plows and rifles.

And the Shawnee came with a vengeance.

That summer, while Mitchell was away, warriors descended on the Clay homestead.

His son Bartley was shot dead in the field.

His daughter Tabitha was stabbed and scalped.

His youngest boy, Ezekiel, was taken. Days later, his scorched corpse was found tied to a stake in the ashes of a Shawnee fire.

The ground never healed.

Joy Built on Bones

In 1926, Conley Snidow thought he could build something better. He paved over the grief with a Ferris wheel and a swimming pond. He turned the site into Lake Shawnee Amusement Park. For a time, it worked. Children swarmed the place. Picnics. Laughter. Birthday candles and summer screams.

Then came the deaths.

A little girl crushed on the swings—Emiline Shrader, killed when a delivery truck reversed into the arc of her joy.

A young boy drowned in the lake, sucked under by a broken drain. His body didn't rise until the next morning.

They say there were more. Some never written down.

Some too awful to retell.

The Graveyard Below

The park closed in 1966. Too many tragedies. Too many whispers. When it was reopened in the 1980s, crews brought back the rides. But when they started digging, they hit bone.

Dozens of skeletons. Mostly children. Archaeologists came. They said it was a burial site. Shawnee. Three thousand graves, they guessed.

The land groaned. And the wind turned colder.

The Ghosts That Linger

Today, the park is overgrown. Rusted. The swing chains rattle even when the air is still. People say they see Emiline—barefoot, bloodstained dress, staring. Some say she swings. Some say she stares.

Others hear sobbing from beneath the soil. Small hands print the windows of the abandoned ticket booth.

Sometimes, a girl is seen walking toward the water— just before she vanishes.

You Can Still Visit

They offer tours now. Halloween ghost hunts. You can pay to walk through the rot. But don't bring children. Don't touch the swings. Don't follow the girl in white.

Because she might not be the only one.

And Lake Shawnee doesn't forget the dead.

It invites more.

Ghost Hollow at the Old Bethany Viaduct
(Brooke County)

"They call it Ghost Hollow, 'cause men it do swallow."

Tunnels, Screams, and Steel

From 1908 to 1926, a trolley cut through the hills between Wellsburg and Bethany—just over seven miles of rattling track that hugged tight turns, skimmed stone tunnels with inches to spare and teetered high above jagged hollows on narrow iron viaducts.

They called it the Wellsburg-Bethany Trolley. A marvel in its day. It carved a path once known only by the old Turnpike—a crooked, mud-choked road where travelers snapped wagon wheels and heard things whisper in the trees.

The trolley felt safer. But it wasn't.

Blood on the Rails

Men died.

One derailed in 1917, flung like a rag from the trolley, and cracked open on Buchannon's Hill. Another, a 75-year-old farmer, was sliced down in the tunnel's throat—his blood staining the stone where no sunlight could dry it.

But there's another death they don't like to speak of. The one that birthed the shadow in the hollow.

A businessman. Dressed fine. Shoes shined. He boarded the trolley with a letter in his pocket, bound for a meeting just past Bethany. But the car lost power crossing the viaduct—an outage. The lights flickered. The car stalled. He stepped off, thinking he'd arrived.

And fell.

Down into the hollow below. The steel did not catch him. Only air. Then stone.

They found him two days later. Back cracked, limbs shattered. His hands still clutched that letter. His eyes still open.

The Hollow That Watches

The trolley's gone now, but the hollow still waits. They call it Ghost Hollow. And the thing inside it is not quiet.

They say he walks the incline where his bones broke, drifting up the slope toward the tracks. His face smeared, grinning wrong. The letter still in hand, though it's rotted and soaked through.

Sometimes, he floats, dusk-colored and silent, eyes like burnt holes staring up at the viaduct. Other times, he stands beside the trees—waiting for someone late to meet him.

They say if you walk the path along the old line, don't stop near the hollow.

Don't speak if you feel someone watching.

Because he hears.

And if you look down into the dark, he might not be looking up.

He might already be beside you.

Tale of William Strange
(Braxton County)

"Strange is my name, and I'm on strange ground, and strange it is that I can't be found."

A Lost Man in the Bones of the Forest

In the fall of 1795, Henry Jackson's surveying crew crept through the raw wilds of what would become West Virginia—thickets around the Elk River still untouched by man. With them rode a supply packer named William Strange. He wasn't a brave or smart man. Just willing. He kept the mules fed, the cookware clean, and his rifle dry.

But one storm-gray afternoon, Strange was sent ahead—alone—with orders to follow the left fork of the Holly River. He was to meet them later, just where the water bled into the Elk. He took the wrong fork.

Nobody knows what happened in those first hours. But when the others reached camp, Strange was gone.

A Hollow Full of Tracks

They found his horse tied to a sapling. Still saddled. Still quiet. Strange's boot prints wandered all around it—circles, zigzags, vanishing and returning again like a man chasing his own ghost. It was as if he'd gotten lost in one single place.

No blood. No signs of a struggle.

Just tracks that led nowhere.

The men fired a single shot to let him know help was coming but feared any more would sound like war cries and drive him deeper into the wilderness.

For two days, they searched. Then they gave up.

Winter took the rest.

The Tree That Speaks

Years later, a hunter stumbled across a narrow ravine and found a rifle jammed into a cleft in the rocks. Bones littered the ground like dropped kindling. Nearby stood a beech tree. On it was a carving: "Strange is my name, and I'm on strange ground, and strange it is that I can't be found."

People laughed at first. Until other hunters saw a pale man beneath that same tree, whispering for help, eyes wide with confusion. His mouth moving without sound.

His clothes rotted. One man claimed the spirit asked him which fork to take, his hand pointing out toward nothing.

The hunter ran. He didn't go back.

Stranger Than Death

It wasn't the first time Strange had lost his way. Reger and Hall—two of his neighbors—remembered a hunting trip years before. They had split up across three ridges. William Strange, green, and clumsy, he was given the easiest route. But when they found him, he was pacing like a trapped hound, unsure which direction was home.

When they told him he was headed the wrong way, he pointed at his own tracks and swore up and down that they led back to the farm.

That had just been a funny story. A dumb neighbor with no sense of direction. Until he vanished. Until the woods took him whole. And never gave him back.

A Warning Carved in Bark

No one agrees where the beech tree stands. Some say the carving fades by day and returns by moonlight. Some claim the ghost wanders now—less confused, more hungry. His eyes are glassy and gray. And when he opens his mouth, the voice is not his own.

The locals won't guide you there. Not anymore. And if you ever hear someone whisper from the woods:

"Which way is the left fork?"

Don't answer. Don't turn.

Just walk away. And pray the trees forget your name.

Because now he's desperate—feral with confusion, frantic to find his way home.

But William Strange isn't a man anymore.

He's become a hollow, ghoulish thing—skeletal and blistered, draped in the stink of rot and snowmelt. A wraith who's worn the woods thin with his circling, and now he's hunting something new:

A skin.

Legs to walk with. Eyes to see the trail.

If you cross him, he might crawl inside you—split you open and wear your body like old clothes, staggering through the brush in your boots with your bones creaking under his weight.

But he'll still be lost. Still walking in blind, endless circles.

And your soul?

It'll be screaming the whole way.

Little Ghouls on the Cacapon
(Hampshire County)

*"They float in tubs with grinning eyes,
and drag you down when the river cries."*

The Tub Boys of Cacapon

The Cacapon River does not begin in any traditional way. It rises from the belly of the earth, spewing forth like something spat up by the dark. Near Wardensville, in the shadow of Sandy Ridge, the river reemerges from a hollowed gap in the limestone—a place where the Lost River vanishes completely beneath the surface as if devoured by some hidden mouth in the mountain.

The Cacapon snakes 81 miles through hills, hollows, and old farmland before spilling into the Potomac. But it never forgets what it swallowed.

And neither does Capon Bridge.

The Picnic That Went Bad

It was the summer of 1892, and the townsfolk were gathered for the yearly church picnic at the bend. Quilts spread across the grass. Bread and molasses. Fried chicken in tin buckets. The preacher's daughters twirling parasols beneath the sycamores. The river sparkled.

Then came the boys' race.

It was a tradition—young boys climbed into old metal washtubs and shoved off upstream, kicking and giggling as the current spun them. A prize was promised for the fastest drift.

But it wasn't the speed that mattered that year.

It was the silence that came after.

One boy, eleven years old, never came back. His name is lost now—some say, Levi, some say Boyd—but all agree the tub was found spinning slowly against a moss-covered rock.

Empty.

The river had taken him.

The laughter stopped. And so did the picnic.

They dragged the river all afternoon. Then into the night. But there was no body.

No trace. Just the gentle gurgling of water rolling over stones like it was chewing.

The next summer, the river gave something back.

What Comes Downstream

It started small.

A fisherman said he saw a face in the current—white, bloated, and smiling.

Then, a couple pulling a skiff felt something slam the side of their boat.

When they looked over the edge, there were two boys in washtubs drifting silently alongside, grinning up, their eyes like marbles, mouths black and open.

The tub boys became legend. Men refused to fish alone. The local children were warned never to swim in the Cacapon, especially not near the old picnic bend.

But they did.

And more tubs appeared.

Some empty.

Some not.

Rowboats would disappear from the banks and be found bobbing in the river, tethered to nothing, rocking gently as if someone—or something—was waiting inside.

Others swore they heard laughter—wet and distant—right before a boat capsized.

More than once, a pale hand reached up from under the water to grab an oar.

And sometimes, too late to scream, a face appeared beneath the surface—smiling, grinning with teeth water-warped and gray.

Still laughing.

Still waiting.

What the River Wants

Now, they say the river keeps count. It took one child but wants more. The current shifts for the tub boys, and where they float, the Cacapon pulls deep and slow like it's breathing.

They come in the dusk now—barely visible except for their white knuckles on rusted washtubs, their bodies stiff and gray with weeds clinging to their shoulders. Some say they try to climb into boats.

Others say they don't need to.

And if you see a child drifting past on the current, don't call to him.

Don't reach for him.

Because he may open his eyes and smile.

And he may not be alone.

You won't see the others until it's too late—pale hands rising from beneath, mouths full of river rot, and the last thing you'll feel is something tugging at your ankles, pulling you into their game.

Because they don't want to be saved.

They want someone new to drown. To ride along with them. Forever.

Witch of Monongah
(Marion County)

*"She taught the girl in whispers low,
then left her doll in death to grow."*

The Hungarian

In the old coal town of Monongah, where dust clings to the windowsills and the smoke of a hundred years never quite leaves the air, a Hungarian woman once lived at the edge of the woods—alone, bent, and quiet.

She kept to herself and rarely spoke except in her native tongue.

Children whispered that she could hex a person by looking at them too long.

Chickens wouldn't go near her gate.

Women crossed themselves when they passed her path to the market.

When she spat at someone's feet, they prayed harder that night, believing it was a sign that she did not want them nearby. They considered it a bad omen, convinced she was spitting away a curse they carried in their soul.

But she wasn't cruel. Only strange. And she had a way of knowing things before they happened.

The townsfolk never gave her a proper name. They simply called her The Hungarian as if that said enough. And in truth, it did.

The Doll with the Heart Pin

Then, one autumn, her garden overgrew, her chimney ceased smoking, and the lights in her house never returned. She had died quietly. Alone, as she lived.

When the town doctor and sheriff entered her crooked little house, they found her curled in her bed—her face twisted in a grimace of peace or pain, it was hard to say. But next to her, on the nightstand, sat a doll.

A crude thing. Stuffed with soot. Threadbare. And pierced straight through the heart with a long, rusted pin.

Rumors grew like vines. But the whispers grew louder when people recalled a girl—twelve, maybe thirteen—who had visited the Hungarian more than once. A curious and precocious girl, not afraid of old wives' tales.

She'd been seen bringing bread and sometimes flowers. And once, someone claimed, she left the house with her palms streaked in ash and her pockets heavy with bone.

The girl changed after that. Her eyes went dull and faraway.

Animals stopped following her the way they once did.

And people began to avoid her the way they had the Hungarian. Because strange things started happening— sickness in houses she passed.

Dead birds at her doorstep.

A dog found dead with its tongue lolling out and foam at his lips.

They say the woman never truly died. She only passed herself on. And if you go to Monongah and find that girl— grown now—you'll see she still walks alone. And sometimes, in the window of her cottage on the edge of the woods, a candle burns behind the silhouette of two women: one old, one young, neither of them moving.

One of them long dead.

The other, waiting.

White Thing
(Marion and Kanawha County)

"It floats behind, but makes no sound—
until your feet leave off the ground.

A Shriek in the Hollow

It was late—too late—for a girl to be riding alone.

She had just left a Saturday revival in the lower Kanawha Valley, the kind where preachers howled and sweat poured like rain.

She was headed home on her dappled mare, the stars burning cold above her, the dirt road veiled in fog.

The trees were like hunched ancient wild things whispering among themselves.

Then it came.

A scream, not human, not animal—something torn and wild, bubbling up from the blackest part of the woods.

The mare froze.

Then it reared so hard she nearly lost the reins. And from the trees, something crawled into the road.

It was white.

White as bone, white as worm-eaten flesh. As tall as the horse, its fur hung in rotted clumps, and its mouth stretched long and torn with teeth like broken needles pointing out in every direction.

It made no sound now—only looked.

Then it ran.

It didn't gallop—it glided. Keeping pace. Just off her stirrups. Its jaws gaped open, unhinged, and inside that mouth, something pulsed.

She screamed. She kicked. The mare bolted down the road, hooves clattering like gunfire on the rock, but still, the White Thing followed—its breath cold, its howl echoing just behind her ears.

Only near the fence post at the edge of the family farm did the thing vanish, slipping back into the dark like a rotten thought.

She threw herself off the saddle, shoved the mare into the barn, and barred the door.

She didn't sleep.

Skin and Screams

By morning, her father found her horse collapsed, jaw twisted in a silent shriek. Its skin peeled clean from muscle like wet paper.

Not eaten. Peeled.

Blood soaked the threshold of the barn. But no tracks led away.

The girl never spoke much after that.

The Thing in the Ridge

Decades later, in the summer of 1929, Frank Kozul—a miner up near Rivesville—cut across the ridges of Morgan's Hollow after a long shift. The air was swampy with heat and gnats, and the only sound was the chink of his lunch pail and the rustle of leaves.

Until something white stepped into the path.

It hovered just above the ground, wide-headed, with a tail like a bristled broom and a body bloated like drowned meat. No face. No eyes.

Frank did what most men would do. He kicked it.

His foot passed through like mist.

Then it lunged.

Frank swung his pail, swung a stick, swung anything he could grab. The Thing tore at him, raked invisible claws across his arms, hissed wet and low against his throat. He ran, stumbling through brush and thorn, and only when he reached the old cemetery did the Thing vanish in a flash of rotted frost.

He reached home, peeled back his sleeves—

And found nothing.

No cuts. No blood. Just the lingering feel of something cold that had touched him without touching at all.

He never walked that ridge again.

Something Still Out There

Others tell of livestock torn open, spines snapped in odd angles, and white fur drifting on the wind. Guns jam. Bullets pass through. And always—that scream.

High, shrill, like metal in the wind.

And in 1994, a man driving through the holler near Fairmont looked out his truck window and saw a white shape keeping pace in the dark. It didn't run. It floated. Hair hung like seaweed. No face. Just a blank canvas and the sense it was smiling.

Then it was gone.

But the scratches showed up on the truck door the next morning.

A Warning on the Wind

They say if you see it—don't stop. Don't speak.

Because it doesn't bleed. It doesn't break.

And it doesn't leave until it takes something.

The Blood on Grasslick Road
(Jackson County)

"In the dark of Grasslick's cursed ground,
he climbs back up when no one's around."

A Kindly Home, Before the Screaming Started

In the late autumn of 1897, Chloe Pfost-Greene lived quietly with her grown children—Jimmy Greene, just eighteen, and her daughters Matilda and Alice Pfost—in a weathered homestead nestled beside Grasslick Creek in Jackson County.

Chloe was known to be generous, too generous maybe.

She gave fresh bread to strangers, housed the hungry. Once, she took in a ragged boy named John Morgan like he was her own.

John had no family. He was just a boy when he showed up, maybe nine or ten, and Chloe fed him, clothed him, and gave him warmth when the world would've let him freeze.

He called her Mama.

She called him son.

But something in John Morgan rotted with time. The boy she saved grew lean and shadow-eyed. Married young, worked when he could, begged when he couldn't.

And whispered to himself when no one was listening.

The First Sign

Just after midnight on October 29th, Morgan crept up the porch like a fox. He rapped on the window and begged Jimmy to come raccoon hunting. Jimmy, half asleep, followed him outside. But before they reached the tree line, Morgan turned to him and asked about the horse they'd been trying to sell.

Jimmy told him it hadn't sold yet.

Morgan just nodded, said nothing, and called off the hunt.

The Slaughter at Grasslick Creek

Four days later, on the evening of November 2nd, John returned.

He asked Chloe for a haircut. She told him to stay the night and she'd take care of it in the morning. That was her mistake.

She didn't see the glint in his eyes. Didn't hear the blood already humming in his ears.

At dawn, Jimmy and John went out to feed the hogs. The cold bit their fingers. The sun hadn't risen.

That's when John grabbed the hatchet.

He brought it down once. Then again. And again. Until Jimmy Greene's skull split like timber, and his body crumpled in the muck.

John left him there.

Then, silent and calm, he walked back into the warm house where Chloe's daughters were making breakfast. Alice stirred batter. Matilda stoked the stove. Chloe was still upstairs, straightening the bed.

He came through the kitchen like a shadow. Brought the blade down on Alice's head. She dropped without a sound. Matilda screamed—but only once before the hatchet caught her twice in the temple. The blade sunk in deep. Blood sprayed the walls.

Then came Chloe.

She fought him. Fought hard. The old woman didn't die easy. He chased her through the house, her screams tearing through the air, until he caught her near the front door. The final blow split her skull wide, and she crumpled in a pool of her own blood.

The One Who Got Away

But Alice wasn't dead. Not yet.

Half-conscious, her scalp hanging loose, she crawled out the back and dragged herself into the henhouse. Matilda screamed her name and begged for the gun.

169

But Alice couldn't go back.

All she could do was run.

She ran down Grasslick Road barefoot, blood pouring down her neck, until she found a neighbor's house and collapsed.

When they returned, they found four bodies. Only three were dead.

He Still Hunts

John Morgan was arrested, tried, and hanged before Christmas. Some say he laughed before they dropped him. Others say he wept like a child. No motive was ever found beyond a thirty-five dollar horse loan.

But that's not the end of it. No.

People say you can still hear Alice running. Still, hear her bare feet slapping the dirt on Grasslick Road. And if you listen, if you really listen, you can hear the others screaming too—Chloe, Matilda, Jimmy—begging her to come back, to help them.

But the worst part isn't the ghosts. It's what still chases her. Some swear John Morgan never stayed buried.

That the ground spat him out. That when the wind goes bitter and the road goes quiet, he pulls himself from the filth—his skin black with rot, his eyes eaten away, his mouth still twisted in that high, cackling giggle.

He walks. Not to find peace. Not for penance.

He walks to chase Alice.

And if you're standing on that road when he comes, if you hear the screaming, you better pray you're not in his way.

Dead Run at Harpers Ferry
(Jefferson County)

"He shot him through and tried to flee,
but now he runs eternally."

Where Smoke Lingers in the Walls

The Harpers Ferry armory sat quiet that January day. Cold. Still. The Potomac was breathing steam. It was 2 p.m. on January 29, 1830, when Thomas B. Dunn stirred the fire in his office like he always did. He had just come back from lunch. Just sat down. Just picked up a book.

Dunn had certain rules. No dice. No drink. No idling.

If your musket failed inspection, you'd feel it in your wages. That made him enemies. He'd fired the old-timers. Turned away drunkards. Raised the bar—and workers hated him for it.

And one of them hated him enough to kill.

The Straw That Meant Death

The plot began in low whispers—bitter muttering from men who once worked the line but had been cast out for being too slow, too drunk, too sloppy with gunmetal.

A handful of them—four or five—started meeting after dark in the corners of taverns and smithies. They grumbled that Dunn was arrogant. A tyrant. A thief of livelihoods. They said the armory would be better off without him.

So they tried. The first attempt was a mess of nerves and wet powder. They dressed in women's clothes, shawls pulled low and crept beneath Dunn's window like rats in skirts. Tried to shoot him through the glass while he read by candlelight. But the air was damp. The gunpowder fizzled. When they pulled the triggers—nothing. Just a weak click and the sound of their own breathing.

They bolted. Stumbling down the street in borrowed petticoats. Cowards.

So they tried again.

They gathered in the dark and cut broom corn stalks—one short, the rest long. Shortest straw would strike the blow.

It was Ebenezer Cox who lost. He got the short straw.

Twenty-one. A drunk. A gambler. Fired from the armory long before Dunn ever arrived and bitter enough to keep the grudge like rot in his bones. His father had kicked him out for drunken rages. The Antietam Ironworks refused to hire him back. He thought woodcutting was beneath him.

He wandered the streets with anger in his teeth, muttering in the blacksmith shop about what he'd do. Told four men he'd ask one last time.

If Dunn said no again—he'd kill him.

They laughed.

He didn't.

The Shot That Rattled the Bricks

Cox walked into the armory with a musket—the name scraped off the stock, the steel cold and hungry. He walked into Dunn's office. The fire was still glowing low.

"You won't give me work?" Cox asked.

"I cannot," Dunn said.

"You're sure?"

"I am."

That was all. Cox lifted the musket. Dunn stood, maybe to stop him. Maybe just too slow.

"My God!" Dunn cried.

The shot cracked the walls. But it wasn't sharp like a pistol. It was deep. Dull. A boom that felt like something inside the building had caved in.

Smoke filled the room. When the clerks rushed in, they found Dunn on his back, bleeding out. His book lay beside him.

The floor was red and slippery. A mess of blood and bile and something white—his stomach, ruptured, spilled into his lap. The wound frothed like a mouth trying to scream. The musket lay a foot from his side.

The Fugitive Ghost

Cox ran. Down Shenandoah Street. His hands crammed in his coat. Eyes wide, mouth working, but no sound came out. He looked over his shoulder like something was chasing him. They found him hunched in the waterwheel house. Cloak over his head. Hiding like a child.

The Hanging

August came hot and cruel. Cox showed no remorse. He told the court that Dunn had vexed him. That he'd been humiliated. Denied work. Denied dignity.

Dozens had seen him enter Dunn's office with a gun. Dozens more had heard him threaten it days before.

He was hanged. The others—those who helped him plan—walked free. But it's Cox who doesn't rest.

The Running Doesn't Stop

They say he still runs Shenandoah Street occasionally scaring those walking at night. Ragged coat flapping. Mouth open in a silent scream. Always heading for the waterwheel. Always looking over his shoulder.

Because something is behind him. Some say it's guilt. Some say it's the law. Some say it is Hellhounds. But old folks say it's Dunn. Still bleeding. Still clutching his stomach. And every night, just after sundown, Cox relives it— the door, the gun, the firelight—and the moment his soul snapped free like a musket's trigger.

Ghosts of Hatfield & McCoy Feud
(Mingo County)

"They rise from graves with boots still red,
to wash their sins but not their dead."

Blood on Both Sides of the River

If not for the feud, they might've just been neighbors.

Just two families living across from each other, the Hatfields on the West Virginia side, the McCoys on the Kentucky.

But the war made animals out of men.

And the land drank what they spilled.

The Hatfields ran timber and sold liquor in Mingo. The McCoys raised hogs in Pike. The war split their bloodlines straight down the Tug Fork. Union blue and Confederate gray. But the killing didn't end in '65. It only got meaner.

The dead didn't stay quiet. And neither did the living.

The First Ghost

Asa Harmon McCoy came home broken. His leg shattered, lungs full of fever. He fought for the Union—alone in a house full of graycoats. Even his own kin glared at him sideways.

Then came the threat: the Logan Wildcats, Devil Anse Hatfield's band of rebel militia, said they were coming.

So Asa ran. Hid in a cave along Blue Spring Creek. Pete, his enslaved servant, brought food, slipping through snow and leaving footprints behind.

On January 7, 1865, those prints were followed. The Wildcats found the cave. A shot rang out. Asa died cold and bleeding, his lungs gurgling with rot and gunpowder.

They never buried him right. And he never left.

They say Asa walks that creek on winter nights. His leg bent wrong. His breath steaming through a hole in his chest. Whispering curses to anyone in Confederate gray.

The Hog That Split the Hills

In 1878, it was a hog that tore the wound wide open again. Randolph McCoy saw the notched ear and said Floyd Hatfield stole it.

Preacher Anse Hatfield, who smelled like sweat and salvation, presided over the trial from his cabin. A cousin swore it was Floyd's hog. The court agreed.

So the McCoys spilled more blood. Sam and Paris McCoy killed the cousin—Bill Staton. Cut him down in a fight.

And once blood hits dirt, it calls for more.

Roseanna's Baby

Roseanna McCoy fled her family's wrath and rode into the arms of Johnse Hatfield. She thought love might end the war.

She was wrong.

She got pregnant. The Hatfields turned on her. The McCoys disowned her. She lost her baby, lost her home, lost her mind.

She died at thirty. And they say her ghost rocks a cradle no one can see, singing lullabies.

The Paw Paw Tree Murders

Election Day, 1882. The blackberry thickets were buzzing with whiskey and rage.

Tolbert McCoy and his brothers stabbed Ellison Hatfield—Devil Anse's kin. Shot him.

Crushed his skull with a stone.

The Hatfields took the boys—dragged them across the Tug Fork to West Virginia. Kept them tied in a clearing full of paw paw trees, their thin trunks swaying like gallows. Ellison lingered for two days before dying. Then the Hatfields lined the McCoy boys up, tied them to trees, and filled them full of lead.

One for each wound Ellison took. One extra to seal the spell.

They say the trees there never grew straight again. And when the wind blows through them, you can still hear the bullets.

The Burning of the McCoy Home

New Year's Night, 1888. Devil Anse's men came like wolves.

They set Randolph McCoy's house on fire—lit it like kindling to burn out the family.

His daughter Alifair, crippled by polio, tried to fetch water. They shot her where she stood.

His son Calvin died in the smoke.

His wife Sarah's skull was caved in by rifle butts.

Randolph escaped with a toddler in his arms—barefoot, running into the trees while his home turned to ash.

Some say Alifair's ghost still drags her limp leg across the clearing, calling for water. But her voice never leaves her throat.

Cotton Top and the Last Rope

They called him Cotton Top—Ellison Mounts. Slow-minded. Easy to sway. The Hatfields handed him the gun, and he obeyed.

He confessed. Then tried to take it back. Didn't matter. He was hanged on February 18, 1890—the last public execution in Kentucky.

His last words were:

"They made me do it. The Hatfields made me do it."

They say his feet didn't kick. Just twitched.

And that something climbed out of him when the rope snapped.

The March of the Dead

They say Devil Anse Hatfield died saved, baptized in the muddy waters of Island Creek. But the mountains remember more than the Bible.

On fog-thick nights, when the moon is low, Devil Anse and his sons rise from their graves. Dirty boots. Blank eyes. Shirts stained with soot and gore.

They march slowly down the mountainside to the same creek where they once baptized blood and bone.

And there—standing waist-deep in the water—Preacher William Garrett waits. He baptizes them again and again, washing the same sins that won't stay gone.

And when the last one is dunked, they vanish. Until the next time.

One by one, the Hatfields and McCoys died. But the feud didn't.

It sleeps in the fog.

It walks the creek beds.

It weeps in the trees.

And sometimes, it kills again.

Dried Bones on Bouge Harman Mountain

(Mercer County)

"If you hear the scream and see the hound—
turn around, run, don't stand your ground..."

The Bones Beneath the Pines

They say you can still hear the screams. Not far from the old trail on Bouge Harman Mountain, where the pines twist, and the soil never seems to thaw, the bones of two lovers were found—picked clean and bleached by sun.

All that remained was a rusted coat button, a patch of blood-dark cloth, and a tangle of long, golden hair. That was Betty Spangler.

A Love That Soured Like Milk in Summer

Betty was poor, but her beauty made men stumble. Hair like sun-warmed wheat. A voice soft as creekwater. She lived on the ragged side of the ridge, in a cabin with patched windows and bitter parents.

Robert Young was the son of a wealthy farmer, clean-fingered, clean-cut, and full of fool hope.

They lived a mile apart and a world away.

Their parents hated each other like fire hates wet wood.

But love doesn't care who hates who.

Betty and Robert swore they'd run.

They packed light. Robert stole two strong horses from his father's barn. Slipped a roll of money in his coat. No moon above, just fog. They were headed to Huntington to be married—young, burning, desperate.

They never made it past the mountain.

Gunfire and Screams in the Hollow

That night, neighbors heard it—

Gunshots cracking the trees.

A scream—high, female, begging.

Then silence thick as blood in snow.

Nobody found them at first. It was months later that two boys cutting through pine logs came across a stink that stopped them cold. Beneath a pile of rotted brush were bones curled together.

One skull still had hair. Long, yellow, matted with dried leaves. Betty's hair.

The law came. Looked. Left.

Nobody was charged.

Nobody spoke.

But folks had their suspicions. And folks had their fears.

The Dog That Carries Her Soul

It started not long after the bones were buried.

Farmers heard it first—screaming in the trees. A woman crying out, her voice climbing up the ridge like smoke. She cried for her lover. Pleaded with someone unseen.

Then: a snarl. A growl.

The crashing of something running.

And from the shadows came the dog.

Not just any dog—a black one. Bigger than a panther. Eyes like live coal. Its tail was long and plumed like a funeral shroud, its mouth red and open.

It would race down the trail from where the screams were heard and vanish into the trees. No prints. No sound. Just cold.

They say that's not a dog at all.

They say it's Betty.

Her soul rides in the beast.

Still running from whoever pulled the trigger.

Still trying to reach Robert.

Still too late.

The Warning

If you're walking the trail and hear a woman scream—don't run toward it.

If you see the black dog with the burning eyes—don't follow it.

Because it doesn't lead you to safety.

It doesn't lead you to love.

It leads you right where they were killed— and some say it doesn't let you leave.

The Strange Case of Sis Linn
(Gilmer County)

*"She walks from the grave with cold in her breath,
still seeking the hand that dealt her death."*

The Murder that Broke the Town

The headline didn't whisper. It screamed.

SARAH LOUISE LINN KILLED IN HER HOME.

The Glenville Democrat, February 20th, 1919, printed in black but read in blood.

They called it the foulest, most blood-thirsty murder ever seen in Gilmer County.

An old Christian schoolteacher, beaten in her bedroom, her Bible cracked open to Ecclesiastes like it had been torn from her dying hands. The page read: "A time to kill and a time to heal…"

There was no healing.

A Lady with a Life and Enemies

Sarah Louise Linn—Sis to those who knew her—was 66 years old. A teacher of 27 years. A woman of books and discipline, scripture and ink. She'd survived a bitter husband and took back her maiden name like a war cry.

Some say she ran a boarding house near the end. Others whispered she had money. Too much for a woman alone. Too much for someone in a house with thin walls and no one to guard her but God.

Blood on the Parlor Floor

On a Saturday night in February, just after 8 p.m., a man named Charles Lewis came knocking—looking for hickory wood. No answer. Just stillness behind the door. No flicker of lamp light.

No voice.

He found her nephew, Howard Brannon, a clerk at Glenville Bank. Asked him if he'd seen Sis. He hadn't.

The two men, joined by others, returned with flashlights and dread. They slipped in through the back, the door yawning open like a broken jaw.

Inside was chaos. Chairs overturned. Tables split. Papers scattered like birds in a storm.

And in the center of the room, on the wood floor, was Sarah Louise Linn.

Her skull had been caved in with a club—still lying nearby, soaked in blood, splintered with bone, and matted with hair.

No One Was Ever Punished

No one was arrested. No one was tried.

The killer vanished like steam in a windy field.

Five years later, the house was demolished. Glenville College bought the lot. They built Verona Mapel Hall, a women's dormitory, right where her parlor once stood.

But Sis Linn wasn't done.

She Would Not Stay Buried

The stories began before the walls were dry.

Trash cans hurled without hands.

Doors slammed in rooms that no one entered.

Chairs dragged across floors by invisible fists.

And always—always—the sound of something moving through her old home... pacing.

When the dorm was torn down in 1978 to make way for a parking lot, the noise didn't stop.

It only spread.

The March of the Murdered

Now they say she haunts all of it.

Clark Hall.

The dorms.

The lot.

The stretch between the cemetery and the classrooms.

They hear her in the walls.

They see lights flicker and die.

They hear the drag of table legs and the snap of doors.

Some students say they've felt breath behind their ears—cold, damp, and sour with old blood.

She's been seen, too.

In 1984, the Bluefield Daily Telegraph reported a white figure walking from the cemetery. Seen only from the waist up at first, her arms swing stiff and slow like a soldier's. As she moves toward the buildings, her lower half fades in—step by step until she's whole.

She makes her way up the lot... always looking forward... never looking back.

A Warning to the Living

If you're on that hill after dark—

If the lights start flickering,

If the furniture shifts and the doors bang open—

Leave.

Because Sis Linn is still searching.

And if you're near the place where her blood dried— she just might mistake you for the one who killed her.

And this time, she's not the one with her back turned.

The Ghost in the Hempfield Tunnel
(Ohio County)

*"Split skull grinning from the ceiling high,
he points and screams, "You too must die."*

The Hatchet Slayer and the Man He Butchered

In June of 1867, the tunnel swallowed a man whole.

His name was Alois Ulrich—a German immigrant with a coin pouch in his coat and a long road behind him.

He was headed east with cash on his belt and calluses on his hands, walking the old line that ran through Hempfield Tunnel just west of Wheeling.

He never made it out the other side.

Waiting in the dark was Joseph Eisele, a man whose soul had already curdled. He was desperate, broke, and full of a killing sort of hunger.

He had a hatchet.

And he had no mercy.

They say the first blow caught Ulrich behind the ear. The second split his scalp like fruit. And by the time it was done, the tunnel walls were slick with blood and the hatchet was red to the hilt.

Eisele left him there—face down in the dirt and crushed rock, his skull cracked open like a boiled egg. He took the money and disappeared into the hills.

But the tunnel didn't stay silent for long.

The Man in the Slime

Weeks passed. Then came the sightings.

At first, just a figure—something leaning in the shadows. A shape that blinked out when approached. Men thought they were tired. Thought they imagined it.

Then came the smell. Like iron and rot and something growing in a wet wound. Decay. Rotten eggs. Death.

Then came the slime.

Railwaymen swore they saw a body stuck to the ceiling, upside down, bathed in green filth that dripped like mucus from a corpse's gut. Its limbs dangled like dead vines, and its eyes were black pits weeping blood.

One hand pointed—a single finger stained red—and from the gash in its head, something pulsed.

And it screamed.

"Let the dead rest!"

"LET THE DEAD REST!"

You Should Pray You Only See the Shadow

Most only ever see the shadow now as they hike through the rail trail tunnel.

A twitch on the tunnel wall. A blur in the corner of your eye. You turn, and it's gone. That's Ulrich... watching.

If that's all you see, you should be grateful.

Because those who've seen the real thing—his split skull, his dripping limbs, the green ooze that follows him like rot in the air—don't sleep right afterward.

Some don't speak.

And a few go missing in the hills.

A Warning for the Tunnel

If you walk the Hempfield Tunnel...

Keep your mouth shut.

Keep your eyes down.

And if you hear screaming from above—

Run. Run. Run. Run. RUN!

Because Ulrich's corpse never made it to a grave.

And the Hatchet Slayer never paid what was due.

So now the tunnel feeds the dead.

And they scream until someone answers.

The Burning Ghost of Frank Easter
(Raleigh County)

"He lit his pipe and fell asleep,
now walks the tracks where embers creep."

Wheedling Out a Ghost Story from Scott Worley

Before he passed, I used to corner David "Scott" Worley every chance I got—Beckley's own ghost hunter. A walking library of Appalachian dread. Folklorist. My go-to person for stories whenever I found myself stuck.

"I need a new one, Scott," I'd say, grinning. "I've dug up every ghost West Virginia has to offer. I'm scraping the bottom of the grave."

Scott would scratch his chin, eyes twinkling behind a serious face.

"Oh, I doubt that," he'd say. "You ever hear about the fire on the tracks? Man's been burning for near a century."

I squinted at him. "You're pulling my leg."

"I kid you not."

He never did, kid.

That was the problem.

A Man Named Frank and a Death Made for Folklore

Frank Easter wasn't much to look at. Quiet man. Coal dust in his teeth, boots scuffed from the Cranberry mines. Lived alone. Ate alone. Drank like he was trying to drown something big.

He'd hitch rides to Beckley—sometimes clinging to the side of freight cars like a ghost already—and wander down Prince Street to lose an evening in liquor and neon. On his way home, he'd follow the rails, mumbling to himself, lighting his pipe to guide the way.

One morning, near the trestle between Beckley and Skelton, another miner caught sight of something glowing on the tracks.

A shape.

Smoldering.

When he got close, he saw it was a body—charred black, steaming in the dawn mist. It was Frank.

No murder. No mystery. They said he'd passed out drunk, pipe still clenched in his teeth. A coal spark had lit him up like a pile of dry leaves. By the time the train crews saw him, he was smoke and cinders.

But Frank Didn't Stay Gone

You'd think that would be the end of it.

But Beckley had other plans.

Not long after, folks started seeing him again.

A figure walking the rails in the dark.

Same coat. Same gait. Same pipe glowing like a little orange eye.

He'd walk to the spot where his body burned.

Then—a flash. Bright as a lightning strike.

Orange and sudden.

Some said it was his ghost reliving the fire.

Some said it was a warning: "Don't stop here. Don't end up like me."

People walking the tracks reported sudden shoves. Pokes in the back. One woman swore someone flicked her ear while she tried to peek down from the trestle.

And here's the kicker—

That spot's still warm.

Even in winter.

Even when the frost creeps up the trees and breath fogs in your lungs.

You press your palm to that stretch of newly surfaced rail trail—it sweats.

I know. I felt it myself.

A Word of Caution

If you're ever on the tracks from Beckley to Skelton—
and you smell smoke but see no fire,

or feel heat rise from cold steel,

or glimpse a glowing dot like a pipe in the dark—keep
walking.

Because Frank Easter's still out there,

burning one step at a time,

looking for a spot to lie down again.

And this time—he might not burn alone.

Citations

- Raw Head and Bloody Bones (Logan and Boone Counties) Origin: Scotch-Irish settlers Sources: WPA folklore projects (1930s), early Boone County oral tradition

- The Hag of Hawk's Nest (Fayette County) Origin: Appalachian witchlore + German "Alp" traditions Sources: WPA oral interviews (1930s), Fayette County Historical Papers (1911)

- The Changeling Child of Cranberry Glades (Pocahontas County) Origin: Scotch-Irish and Acadian French superstition Sources: WPA folklore, Tales of the Central Appalachians (rare 1938 printing)

- The Project Gutenberg eBook, The Fairy Changeling and Other Poems, by Dora Sigerson

- The Wailing Woman of Booger Hole (Clay County) Sources: Clay County Courier archives (1917), oral interviews (1930s)

- The Coal Hollow Lights (Logan and Mingo Counties) Origin: Welsh mining traditions (ghost lights) Sources: Mining folklore, Ghost Tales from Coal Country (out-of-print 1941)

- Black Lucy's Curse (Greenbrier County) Origin: Blend of Appalachian and African-American oral tradition Sources: WPA narratives, Greenbrier Ghost oral archives

- The Specter at Sugar Grove (Pendleton County) Origin: German "Doppelgänger" beliefs blended with frontier superstition Sources: Pendleton County Chronicles (early 1900s), local interviews

- Old Man Fire-Eyes (Nicholas County) Origin: Appalachian devil tales + French Acadian trickster myths Sources: WPA folklore collections (1930s), out-of-print book Tales from the Hills (1935)

- The Blood-Cursed Boy of Mudlick Hollow (Lincoln County) Origin: Hungarian immigrant folklore with Appalachian death lore Sources: WPA folklore project (1930s), coal camp oral tradition

- The Eyes in the Laurel (Greenbrier County) Origin: Appalachian settler superstition, changeling folklore Sources: Oral accounts from the Big Draft wilderness area; WPA-era hunting camp interviews (unpublished field notes/ Oral accounts from Big Draft area hunters; WPA-era forest tales)

• Twistabout Ridge (Procious, Clay County – Local oral tradition, early 1900s–1940s) Origin: Appalachian folk hauntings, Civil War murder tales, and maternal ghost curses Sources: Community oral histories, WPA-style interviews, and regional recollections Twistabout Ridge; The Charleston Daily Mail, Charleston, West Virginia, July 27, 1971 - Page 1 Mountain Lore Warnings Heeded Tall Tale Tellers, Workman, Patricia Samples Between Twistabout and Dismal: Flying Dogs and Ghost Frogs at the Haunted Mud Hole

• Widow Ratliff's Fence (Raleigh County) Origin: Appalachian folk magic and superstition Sources: WPA field notes by R.S. Carpenter, local oral histories (1890s–1930s)

• The Knockers of Buffalo Ridge (Putnam County, West Virginia) Origin: Scotch-Irish mining superstition, Welsh folktales Sources: Coal miner oral histories (1930s WPA), regional accounts from Buffalo Ridge shafts

• Miss Cranley's Mirror (Mason County, West Virginia – Early 1900s) Origin: French Acadian death-lore, Appalachian boarding house superstitions Sources: Regional oral tradition, post-WPA hauntings

• The Lantern Man of Tug Fork (Mingo County, West Virginia – Early 20th Century) Origin: Appalachian miner folklore, ghost light traditions, coalfield death lore Sources: WPA American Life Histories (search "ghost lights" or "phantom miners"), Library of Congress ghost stories archive, regional oral traditions from Tug Fork Valley

• The Cabin That Bled (Greenbrier County, West Virginia – Early 1900s) Origin: Blood-stain hauntings, murder lore, Appalachian house curses; Sources: WPA Federal Writers' Project Archive, Goldenseal Magazine, regional Greenbrier folklore

• The Hollow-Eyed Watcher of Dead Man's Curve (Raleigh County, West Virginia – Mid-20th Century) Origin: Death omens, Appalachian roadside hauntings, fatal crash lore Sources: Library of Congress Folklife Collections

• The Coal Witch of Cabin Creek (Kanawha Valley, West Virginia Late 1800s to Early 1900s) Origin: Appalachian witchcraft, coalfield superstition, folk survival magic Sources: WPA Collections

Witchcraft in Appalachian Folklore– Witch Signs and Miners, WVU archives – West Virginia Folklore Journal (Cabin Creek)

• Kenny, H. (1945). West Virginia place names: Their origin and meaning, including nomenclature of the streams and mountains.

• The Baby That Was Never Born (McDowell County, West Virginia – Early 1900s) Origin: Ghost children, stillbirth superstition, missing burial folklore Sources: Federal Writers' Project – Ghost Children and Burial Superstitions, American Folklife Center – Appalachian Death Lore

• The Woman in the Root Cellar (Mason County– Turn of the Century) Origin: Family hauntings, jealous ghosts, trapped spirit traditions Sources: WPA Folklore Files – Possession and Jealous Ghosts, Library of Congress – Haunted Homes & Family Ghosts

• The Dog That Dug Up the Preacher (Clay County, West Virginia – Early 1900s) Origin: Corpse disturbance, hellhounds, religious folklore Sources: Goldenseal Magazine – Clay County Folklore, Library of Congress – Appalachian Burial Lore, WPA "Superstitions" interviews (LOC WPA Records)

• The Eye in the Creek (Fayette & Nicholas County 1920s–1930s) Origin: Water spirits, death omens, Appalachian superstition Sources: American Folklife Center – Appalachian Water Spirits, LOC Folklore Guide – Ghosts in Natural Settings, WPA Interview Excerpts on Haunted Springs

• The Wizard Clip (Jefferson County– 1790s) Origin: Poltergeist, religious punishment, folk exorcism Sources: WPA West Virginia Folklore Project, American Catholic Historical Researches (Vol. 5, 1909), West Virginia Encyclopedia – "Wizard Clip"; Quackenbush, J. (2018). West Virginia ghost stories, legends, haunts, and folklore.

• The Witch Ball at Hanging Rock (Roane County, West Virginia – Early 1900s) Origin: Curse removal, witchcraft defense, Appalachian folk healing Sources: WV Folklore Collection – Witchcraft Remedies Section, WPA Herbalism Notes – Roane County, 1939

• Falling Run Hanging Tree (Monongahela County, West Virginia) Origin: Corpse disturbance Quackenbush, J. (2018). West Virginia ghost stories, legends, haunts, and folklore.

- The Hand Behind the Door West Virginia Folklore Journal – Vol. 2, "Haunted Homes of the Coal Camps" WPA Folklore Project – Wyoming County, WV ghost stories Appalachian Oral History Collection – Shepherd University Archives   Origin: Accidental murder, guilt haunting, hidden corpse Sources: WPA Folklore Reports – Wyoming County, West Virginia; West Virginia Folklore Journal, 1929; Appalachian Ghost Lore Archive

- Lantern Man WPA Kentucky Ghost Stories – Pike County Mining Camps Journal of Appalachian Superstitions, 1938 edition Eastern Kentucky Oral History Project – "Light Signs of Death" Origin: Appalachian mining camp lore, death omens, unblessed dead Sources: WPA Interviews – Kentucky Division; Journal of Appalachian Superstitions; EKU Oral Folklore Archives

- The Procession: -The Ghost Story: The Wheeling Sunday register (Wheeling, W. Va.). 1885-02-15

- White Bird of Death-Origin: European immigrant folklore, death omens, sacrificial pacts Source: Musick, Ruth Ann. Green Hills of Magic: West Virginia Folktales from Europe. University Press of Kentucky, 1970, pp. 45–47.

- The Chain Musick, R. A., & Musick, A. L. (1977). Coffin Hollow and Other Ghost Tales. University Press of Kentucky. Terry Ann Bradley, Mannington, 1963, as told to her by her grandfather.

- Stretchers Neck- Origin: Theme: Appalachian Tragedy / Ghost Lovers / Betrayal / Death Haunt Basil W. Duke, George Braden Fetter & Shober. (1892). Jim, The Ghost of Stretcher's Neck. Fetter's Southern Magazine,Volume 1.   Brown, L. (n.d.). The Ghosts of Stretchers Neck, Fall 1998. Goldenseal, 64.

- Collins Betts Farm--Cincinnati Enquirer, April 3, 1886   The Haunted House at Grantsville, on the Little Kanawha...

- Ghost of Gamble Run: History of Wetzel County, West Virginia By John C. McEldowney Low Gap. Musick, R. (1965).

- The Murdered Merchant's Ghost. #64 In The Telltale Lilac Bush and Other West Virginia Ghost Tales (pp.96). Univ Press of Ky.

- Ikey's Tomb: -Mt. Welcome cemetery, Pleasants Countywvgenweb.org/pleasants/cemetery/mtwlcm.htm;

Quackenbush, J. (2020). West Virginia ghost stories: The classics.

• Fairmont Headless Brakeman: Musick, R. A. (1965). The telltale lilac Bush: And other West Virginia ghost tales. University Press of Kentucky. The Headless Man

• Coed Murders: Appalachian Mysteries: The Coed Murders by Sarah James McLaughlin, 2021 Interviews/files referenced in "The WVU Coed Murders" podcast, Rod Everly interviews. West Virginia State Police and archival coverage of the 1970 investigation. National Guard report/search logs from Goshen Road recovery site

• Lake Shawnee: Eyewitness accounts and family records from the Clay homestead Local interviews collected by the West Virginia Folklife Program/ Archaeological reports from Marshall University on Lake Shawnee excavation

• E-yearbook Bethany college - Bethanian yearbook (Bethany, WV). Bethany_College_Bethanian_Yearbook/1943/

• William Strange: Creek Whispers Tale of Long Lost Pioneer. (1927, April 2). Charleston Daily Mail.

• Cacapon River Ghost: Crites, S. (1992). Lively Ghosts Along the Potomac -The Rowboat

• Witch of Monongah: Musick, R. A. (1952). Omens and Tokens of West Virginia. Midwest Folklore, 2(4), 263-267. Musick, Ruth Ann. "Witchcraft and the Devil in West Virginia." Appalachian Journal, vol. 1, no. 4, 1974, pp. 271–76.

• Pfost Family: Quackenbush, J. (2017). West Virginia ghost stories, legends, and haunts. 21 Crows Dusk to Dawn Publishing; Morrison, O.J.Slaughter of the Pfost-Greene family of Jackson county

• Harpers Ferry (Harpers Ferry, WV – 1830) Origin: Murder, vengeful ghost, federal armory haunting Sources: U.S. Congressional Serial Set (1830s), Jefferson County Court Records, Local Oral Tradition, WPA Ghost accounts) W.Va. A history of the tragedy; Quackenbush, J. (2018). West Virginia ghost stories, legends, haunts, and folklore. Cincinnati, Ohio: 21 Crows Dusk to Dawn Publishing.

• Hatfields and McCoys: (Tug Fork Valley – 1865–1890s) Origin: Feuding families, ghostly revenants, murder, betrayal, war-haunted land Sources: Appalachian oral tradition, court records, historical newspapers, WPA ghost tales, Hatfield & McCoy family accounts West Virginia Division of Culture and History Archives National Register of Historic Places; Quackenbush, J. (2017). West Virginia ghost stories, legends, and haunts. 21 Crows Dusk to Dawn Publishing

• Black Dog of Bouge Harman Mountain (Logan County– 1800s) Origin: Doomed lovers, ghost dog, Appalachian banshee Sources: Oral tradition, mountain family lore, regional legend)

• Sis Linn: facebook.com/ghostsofwestvirginia/posts/a-haunting-in-glenville-the-front-page-of-the-thursday-february-20th-1919-glenvi/153210518647175/

• The Ghost in the Hempfield Tunnel (Wheeling, West Virginia – 1867) Origin: Murdered traveler, vengeful ghost, tunnel haunting Sources: Local oral tradition, 19th-century crime reports, railway folklore)

• David "Scott" Worley, Founder of Haunted Beckley, ghost hunter, folklorist, and just one of the nicest and most knowledgeable persons I have met.